MEANT FOR ME

SIERRA CARTWRIGHT

HAWKEYE

DEDICATION

Jennifer and Bev, this one could not have happened without you!
For Whit, whose love fills my heart.
For Jaime and the two a.m. check-in!
A special acknowledgment for Shannon, who makes all the things possible.
For you, for sharing your stories and time with me. I appreciate you more than you will ever know.

PROLOGUE

HAWKEYE

"What do you think?"

From his place on the raised platform that had once served as a fire outlook post, Torin Carter glanced at Hawkeye, his boss and mentor. The man owned the security firm Torin worked for, as well as this eight-hundred-acre outpost in the remote part of the West. "Think of what? The class?"

Six times a year, recruits new to the VIP protection program cycled through the Aiken Training Facility. It wasn't Torin's job to get them through. It was his job to make sure that everyone, except the very best, washed out.

"That recruit in specific. Going through the bog." Aviator glasses shaded Hawkeye's eyes as well as his thoughts.

"Mira Araceli?" Torin asked.

"That's the one."

Carrying a thirty-pound pack, face smeared with mud, her training uniform soaked, Mira Araceli dashed at full-out speed toward the next obstacle. She grabbed the rope and began to pull herself up the ten-foot wall as if she hadn't just navigated a killer course designed to destroy her energy reserves.

Today, her long-black hair with its deep fiery highlights was not only in a ponytail, it was tucked inside her jacket. She concentrated on the task in front of her, never looking away from her goal.

Torin had been running the training program for several years. During that time, only a few recruits stood out. "She's…" He searched for words to convey his conflict. Brave. Relentless. Driven, by something she'd never talked about during the admission process.

On a couple of occasions, he'd studied her file. Hawkeye's comprehensive background check had turned up nothing out of the ordinary. Youngest of three kids. Her father was a congressman and former military. Both of her brothers had followed his legacy—and expectations?—into the service.

Araceli's academic scores were excellent. She'd graduated in the top of her college class but had opted not to put her skills to use in a safe corporate environment. Instead, she'd applied to be part of Hawkeye Security, even though she knew the scope of their work, from protecting people and things, to operating in some of the most difficult places on the planet. *Why does she want to put her life at risk?*

Fuck. Why did anyone?

Hawkeye cleared his throat.

Torin glanced back at his boss. "She's one of the most determined I've ever seen. Works harder than anyone. Longer hours." Yesterday he'd hit the gym at five a.m. She was already there, wearing a sports bra beneath a sheer gray tank top. Rather than workout pants, she opted for formfitting shorts that showed off her toned legs and well-formed rear. They exchanged polite greetings, and she'd wandered over to be his spotter for his bench presses, then offered a hand up when he was done.

He shouldn't have accepted. But he had. A sensation, dormant for years, had sparked. Raw sexual attraction for Mira Araceli had shot straight to his cock, a violation of his personal ethics.

She hadn't pulled away like she should have. Her palms were callused, and so much smaller than his. Torin was smart enough to recognize her danger, though. He'd honed her strength himself. She would have him flat on his back anytime she wanted.

In the distance, a door slammed, and they moved away from each other. From across the room, he saw her looking at her hand.

No doubt she'd experienced the same electric pulse as he did.

Since that morning, he'd been damn sure she wasn't in the gym before he entered. Relationships among Hawkeye operatives weren't expressly forbidden. Hawkeye was smart enough to know that close quarters, adrenaline, fear, and survival instincts were a powerful cocktail. But the relationship between a recruit and instructors was sacred.

Having sex with Araceli wouldn't just be stupid—it would border on insane.

In addition to the fact that he was responsible for her safety, Araceli was far too young for his carnal demands. And it wasn't just in terms of age. Life had dealt him a vicious blow, leaving parts of him in jagged pieces.

He no longer even pretended to be relationship material.

When he could, he went to a BDSM club. There, he found women who wanted the same things he did. Extreme. Extreme enough to round the edges off the memories, the past.

There was no way he would subject a recruit to the danger that he represented, even if she was tempting as hell.

Hawkeye was still waiting, and Torin settled for a nonanswer. "Her potential is unlimited."

"But?" Hawkeye folded his arms. Despite the thirty-seven-degree temperature, he'd skipped a coat and opted for a sweatshirt to go with his customary black khakis. Combined with his aviator glasses and black ball cap embroidered with the Hawkeye logo, the company owner was incognito.

Torin looked at her again. "She does best in situations where she is by herself." And that wasn't how Hawkeye Security operated. They believed no person was better alone than as part of a team. Certainly there were times when an agent had no backup and was left with no choice but to take individual action. But the ability to work with others was crucial to success.

"What do you think of her chances?"

Torin shrugged. When she first joined Hawkeye a year ago, she'd trained at the Tactical Operations Center. She could pump thirty-seven out of forty shots into a target's heart and was first through the door during hostage rescue exercises. Though she'd excelled, she took unnecessary risks. At times, she calculatingly ignored superiors' commands. So far it had worked well for her, much to the annoyance of her numerous instructors.

On her application to the program that Torin headed, she'd indicated she had too much downtime during her assignments. She wanted something more demanding. VIP protection could provide that. If she made it.

Araceli summited a second wall, then leaped off and kept moving, dropping down to crawl through a tunnel, then back up to navigate the ridiculously tough agility course.

Hawkeye watched her progress. "There's something about her."

At the end of the course, she doubled over to catch her

breath; then she checked her time on a fitness watch. Only then did she shrug off the pack.

"Lots of potential," Torin agreed.

"Either hone it or get her out of here." Hawkeye adjusted his ball cap. "They'd be glad to have her back in tactical. And with her IQ scores, she'd do well in a support role. Strategy."

She was a little young for that.

Then again, age wasn't always a factor. He knew that more than most.

"You doing okay?" Hawkeye asked.

Torin twitched. "It's easier."

In his usual way, Hawkeye remained silent, letting time and tension stretch, waiting.

"I think about it every day." Dreams. Nightmares. Second-guessing himself, his reactions, replaying it and never changing the outcome.

"You've accumulated plenty of time off."

"I'd rather work."

"Understood."

Torin and Hawkeye watched a couple more recruits finish the course. Results were fed through to his high-tech tablet. Not surprisingly, Mira had finished in the top three.

In the distance, an old bus lumbered toward them, spewing a cloud of dirt in its wake.

Turning his head to watch it, Hawkeye asked, "You heading to Aiken Junction?"

"Yeah." Torin grinned. Drills in the mock town were one of his favorite parts of being an instructor. And he fully intended to use the opportunity to be sure Araceli learned a valuable lesson. "Want to join us?"

"If I had time." Hawkeye sighed. "Another damn dinner. Another damn meeting with a multinational company." Hawkeye wasn't just the founder and owner of the security firm—he was their best performing salesperson. "And I'm going to get the account."

"Never doubted you, boss."

Hawkeye clapped Torin on the shoulder. "I've taken enough of your day."

After nodding, Torin descended the steps, then jogged over to the finish line where recruits were talking, drinking water, dreaming about a beer or the hot tub. "Listen up!"

Talking ceased.

"You're responsible for protecting the family of an important diplomat. Their youngest daughter is seventeen and just slipped her security detail. And you're going to get her back."

There were groans and resigned sighs. The group had hit the running track at six a.m., had hours of classroom instruction, missed lunch, and been timed on their run through the mud challenge. And their day was just beginning.

He pointed to the approaching vehicle. "Gear up."

Exhausted recruits picked up the packs they'd just shucked.

"The bus will stop for ninety seconds. If you're not on it, you'll be hiking to Aiken Junction."

Mira grabbed a protein bar from her bag then slung it over one shoulder. She made sure she was first on the bus and moved to a seat farthest in the back.

Torin jumped on as the driver dropped the transmission into gear. While others had doubled up and were chatting, Araceli leaned forward and draped a T-shirt over her head. Smart. She was taking time to recover mentally and physically.

"Here's the drill." He stood at the top of the stairwell, holding on to a pole as the ancient vehicle hit every damn rock and pothole, jarring his jaw. "The tattoo parlor denied her because she's underage, and the artist we interviewed said he saw her move over to Thump, the nightclub next to

Bones." The name of their fictitious high-end steakhouse. "She has a fake ID, so it's possible she got past security. Her daddy wants her home, and wants her safe. This isn't the first time she's slipped her detail. You'll stage at the church. Choose a team leader and make a plan. Any questions?"

Most people lapsed into silence, a few engaged in banter and trash talk, and he took a seat behind the driver.

A mind-numbing thirty minutes later, the bus churned through Hell's Acre, the seedy area of town, then crossed the fake railroad tracks that separated the sleazy area of town from the more respectable suburban setting.

The driver braked to a grinding halt in front of the clapboard All Saints Church.

"Not so fast," Torin said when the recruits began to stand. "This isn't your stop."

He jogged down the steps to the sidewalk, and the driver pulled the lever to shut the door, then hit the accelerator fast enough to cause the occupants some whiplash—good training for real-life evasive driving. The recruits would be taken around the town several times in order to give Torin and the role-players time to set up.

Once the bus disappeared from view, he pulled open the door to the restaurant and entered the dining room where he greeted fellow instructors. "Who's playing our principal?"

"That's me, Commander." Charlotte Bixby—four feet eleven, ninety-two pounds, and ferocious as a man twice her size—waved from the back of the room. She wore a black dress and flats that would give her some maneuverability.

"And your gentlemen friends?"

Two agents raised their hands.

Torin went through the rest of the roles, couples, bartenders, cocktail servers, DJ Asylum, partiers on the dance floor. All in all, over two dozen people were assigned to the scene. "Okay, people! Let's head over."

Twenty minutes later, music blared. Charlotte was seated in a booth attached to the far wall. She was wedged between two solid men, a cocktail in front of her. The dance floor in the center of the room was filled with gyrating couples, servers moved around the room, and a bartender was drawing a beer. The surveillance room was being manned by one of the instructors, and he was wearing a polo shirt that identified him as one of Thump's security team. The bouncer, nicknamed Bear, was dressed similarly, but wearing a jacket that emphasized his broad shoulders and beefy biceps. Arms folded, Torin stood behind Bear.

Since a cold front was moving through and the temperature had dropped to just above freezing, a coat check had been set up near the front door, close to the restrooms.

Everything was in place.

A role player sashayed through the front door and gave Bear a once-over and an inviting smile. That didn't stop him from scrutinizing her ID.

"Enjoy your evening, Miss."

After snatching her ID back, she breezed past them and headed straight for the bar.

Several more people entered, and none of them were Hawkeye recruits. Hopefully that meant they were still strategizing. He preferred that to seeing them head in without a plan...like they had last time they ran a similar drill.

He checked his watch.

Fifteen minutes.

Then thirty.

Charlotte was on her second cocktail.

An hour.

Torin left the door to grab a beer at the bar. Then he carried it to the side of the room and stood at a tall round table.

DJ Asylum turned on pulsing colored strobe lights and cranked up the music. The walls echoed from the bass. People shouted to be heard.

Exactly like an ordinary bar in Anytown, USA.

One of Charlotte's companions signaled for another drink and then draped that arm across her back. She leaned into him.

Within minutes, Araceli strolled in. Her face was clean, and she'd changed into clean clothes—obviously they'd been in her backpack, along with a shiny headband. Nothing could hide her combat boots, though.

Life wasn't a series of perfect opportunities. Blending in mattered, but speed was critical. It did mean that the role players had an advantage, though.

Along with a fellow trainee, Araceli found a table. Instead of waiting for a cocktail waitress, she headed to the bar. She scanned the occupants, saw him, gave no acknowledgment that they'd ever met.

Yeah. Hawkeye was right. She was damn good.

She secured two drinks, then, instead of heading back to the table, walked to the far end of the room and began a search for their principal.

Smart. She wouldn't approach right away, she'd make sweep, assess the situation, all the while looking as if she fit in.

Except for those ridiculous combat boots.

Under the flashing lights, he lost her. Until her headband winked in the light.

He checked out the other recruits and their strategies. Two of them—women—looped arms like besties and pretended to look for men.

DJ Asylum's voice boomed through the room, distorted by some sort of synthesizer. "Get on the floor and show me your moves!"

One of the trainers walked to the table where Charlotte sat and whispered into the ear of the man with his arm draped over her shoulder.

Araceli put down her drink.

The companion nodded and moved his arm to reach into his pocket. Money exchanged hands.

The second guy slid off his seat, effectively blocking the pathway to the booth.

The man Charlotte was cozying up to led her to the dance floor. Araceli stood, looked around for a male agent, grabbed him, then pulled him toward the other couple.

Moments later, fog spilled from machines, clouding the air.

Lights went out, and the music stopped so abruptly that it seemed to thunder off the still-pulsating walls.

It took a few seconds for emergency lighting to kick on. When it did, the fog was thick and surreal, and Charlotte and her dance partner were gone.

Araceli headed toward the exit and shoved her way past Bear and out of the building.

Torin strolled toward the coatroom. He pushed the door most of the way closed, leaving a crack so he could watch the front door.

Moments later, Araceli hurried back in, her winking headband all but a neon sign indicating her position. He eased the door open, then, as she started past, reached out, grabbed her, pulled her in, and caught her in a rear hold, an elbow under her chin, his right arm beneath her breasts.

She was breathing hard, but she grabbed his forearms to try to break free. In response, he tightened the hold to ward off an elbow jab. And he leaned her forward to prevent one of her vicious, calculated stomps. "Knock it off, Araceli," he growled into her ear.

"Commander Carter?" She froze. "It's dark. How did you know it was me?"

"Your headband."

"Shit."

"That's right. You lose." He loosened his grip slightly, but she kept her hands in place. "Your target is gone."

With a deep, frustrated sigh, she tipped her head back, resting it on his chest. And he noticed her. The way she fit with him, and how she trusted him, despite her annoyance at having been bested. And even the way she smelled…wildflowers and innocence, despite the grueling ordeal earlier today. He wanted to reassure her, let her know how proud he was of her efforts.

Jesus. Immediately he released her. He'd held her longer than he need to. Longer than he should have. "Go to Bones. I'll meet you there." Torin took a step back, literal as well as mental.

In the near dark, she faced him. "But I can—"

"Go. I'm one of the bad guys, Araceli." And not just for the role-playing scenario. He was no good for her. "I took you out of the game. You never even noticed me. You didn't make a plan. You rushed forward without assessing the situation. You failed."

After a few seconds of hesitation, she nodded. "It will be the last time, Commander Carter. You underestimate me and my capabilities."

Something he didn't want to name snaked through him.

She had to be talking about the job, nothing more. Araceli couldn't know about his inner turmoil and his dark attraction to her.

Alone in the dark, Torin balled his hand into a fist over and over, opening, closing. Opening. Closing.

By far, Mira Araceli was the most dangerous student he'd ever had.

CHAPTER ONE

HAWKEYE

"You all right, Mira?"

For three years, six months, and twelve days, Torin Carter had haunted Mira Araceli's days and teased her nights.

Jonathan, the personal trainer she worked with when she was staying in New Orleans, snapped his fingers in front of her face. "Mira?"

His proximity, along with the sharp sound, finally broke through her runaway thoughts, and she shook head to clear it of the distraction that was her former Hawkeye instructor.

What the hell was wrong with her? She shouldn't have checked out mentally, even for a fraction of a second. In the wrong circumstances, it could mean the difference between survival and death. "Sorry." With a smile meant to be reassuring, she met his eyes.

For most of her life, she'd practiced yoga. Five years ago, she'd learned to meditate. Yet when it came to Torin, she never remembered to use her skills.

"Something on your mind?"

"*Was.* There was. I'm good to go now." She was almost

done with the final set—squatting over two hundred pounds. She could do this. *Right?* In a couple of minutes, she'd be out of here and headed for the house where she would spend the next nine weeks living with her nemesis.

How the hell had this even happened? Hawkeye required all instructors—even the head of the program—to spend time in the field to keep their skills sharp. But for them to be assigned to the same team…?

"Ready?" Jonathan asked. "You have three more reps."

With single-minded focus, she tucked way thoughts of her demanding and mysterious former instructor.

Jonathan scowled. "You sure everything's okay?"

She got in position, adjusted her grip, then took a breath.

"Hold up." He nudged one of her feet.

"Thanks." After executing the squat, watching her form, breathing correctly, she racked the bar and stepped away. No matter what she wanted to believe, thoughts of Torin had wormed past her defenses to dominate her thoughts. "I'm calling it."

Jonathan nodded. "Good plan." He checked his clipboard. "See you back the day after tomorrow?"

"Six a.m. I won't miss it." She grabbed her water bottle, took a swig, then headed for the locker room. This was the first time in her adult life that she'd cut a workout short.

Mira showered, then took longer than normal with her makeup. Long enough to piss her off. Frustrated, she shoved the cap back onto her lipstick and dropped it in her bag.

Even though she routinely had male partners, she wasn't in the habit of primping. Of course, she'd never had an all-consuming attraction to one of them before.

Torin Carter wasn't just gorgeous. As her VIP Protective Services instructor, he'd been tougher on her than anyone ever had been, demanding her very best, harshly grading her work. It was his job to make her a stellar agent or cut her from the program. He hadn't known that failure was never a possibility.

During her training, he'd never shown anything beyond a hard-ass, impersonal interaction toward her. Except for that night at Thump.

When he'd caught her in that choke hold, she'd struggled, elbowing him, attempting to stomp on his foot. His commanding voice had subdued her, and when she stopped struggling, she noticed his arms around her.

Even though he loosened his hold, Torin didn't release her right away like other instructors had. And in a reaction that was wholly unlike her, she tipped her head back and relaxed into him, seeking comfort, a brief respite from the relentless and grueling training exercises. For a moment, she forgot about her job, stopped noticing the fog and pandemonium around them.

She thought—maybe—that he experienced an echoing flare, but he pushed her away, with a harsh indictment of her skills.

Drowning in rejection and embarrassment, she squared her shoulders and locked away her ridiculous unrequited emotions and vowed never to examine them again.

Even though she'd graduated years ago and hadn't heard his name since, he was never far away. Frustratingly, she thought of him every time she went out on a date. It was as if her subconscious was weighing and measuring all men against him.

The comparisons even happened when she scened at a BDSM club.

Torin was everything she wanted a Dom to be—uncompromising, strong, intelligent…and, at the right time, reassuring. In his arms, in that coatroom, she'd discovered he was capable of tenderness. Maybe if she'd only seen him be an ass, he would have been easier to forget.

Surviving Torin might be her greatest test ever.

Mira dragged her hair back over her shoulder and stared at herself in the mirror. "You." She pointed at her reflection. "You're smarter this time. Wiser. More in control."

A blonde emerged from one of the shower stalls. "Man problems?"

Embarrassed, Mira lifted a shoulder. She hadn't realized her words would be overheard.

"Isn't it always?" the woman asked.

For other people, not her. "That's the thing. It never has been until now."

"I see you here all the time. You're tough. Whatever it is, you can handle it."

Mira hoped so. She smiled at the other woman. "Thank you. I needed that pep talk." After blotting her lipstick, she gathered her belongings, exited the gym, then strode across the parking lot to her car.

She and Torin were scheduled to rendezvous at seven p.m. at Hawkeye's mansion in the Garden District. Since it was equipped with modern security both inside and out, he preferred his high-value clients utilize it when they visited NOLA. In addition to eight bedrooms, there was a spacious carriage house apartment for use by security personnel.

The grounds were spectacular, with a large outdoor swimming pool, a concrete courtyard with plenty of lounge chairs, tables, and umbrellas. Potted plants provided splashes of color, while numerous trees offered privacy as well as shade.

She'd stayed on the property several times, including earlier this year for Mardi Gras while she was working the detail for an A-list actor. She planned to arrive before Torin so she could select her bedroom, get settled, have the upper hand. Any advantage, no matter how small, was a necessity.

Since it was still early afternoon, she managed the traffic

with only the usual snarls.

After passing the biometric security system at the gate, she drove onto the property.

More confident now, she grabbed her gear, then jogged up the stairs to enter the code on the keypad. A moment later, the lock turned, and she opened the door.

Torin stood in the middle of the main living space, arms folded, damn biceps bulging. His rakishly long black hair was damp, and the atmosphere sizzled with his scent, that of crisp moonlit nights. He swept his gaze over her, and it took all her concentration to remain in place as he assessed her with his shockingly blue eyes.

When he tipped his head to the side, reaction flooded her. Her knees wobbled, and she dropped her duffel bag off her shoulder and lowered her gear to the hardwood floor to disguise her too-real, too-feminine reaction.

His jaw was set, his mouth compressed. There was no way to tell what he was thinking.

How the hell had he arrived before she had? For her not to have seen his car, he must have parked it in the garage. She gave a quick, smart nod, being as stoic as he was. "Commander Carter."

"At present, we're partners. So make it Carter. Or Torin."

Not a chance. No way was she allowing herself to be on intimate terms with him.

Mira turned to close the door and dragged in a deep breath. She was early. Hours and hours early, yet he had the upper hand. As always. Before facing him, she exhaled, focusing on controlling her pulse rate.

"I took the first bedroom."

Not having any other choice, she nodded. "I'll bunk in the back one." Which left an empty one between them

"The fridge is stocked, and so is the pantry, but I figured we'd go to the grocery store together for additional items."

"I'll give you a list of what I need."

"Still not a team player, Araceli?"

Fuck you. "Still critiquing every little thing I do, Carter?" She squared her chin. She'd passed every one of his damn tests.

"Your loss." He shrugged. "I was going to buy you dinner while we were out. There's a place in the French Quarter, on Chartres Street. Their Taste of New Orleans platter is divine."

He was a foodie?

"Crawfish étouffée, gumbo, jambalaya. And a loaf of fresh hot bread."

Damn him, he'd named some of her favorite dishes. Eating was one of the reasons she'd asked to work out of the Southern office. And when she'd received her assignment, she'd bought a house nearby.

"Up to you." He lifted one shoulder in a casual shrug. "Can't starve yourself while you're here."

Eat when you can. Sleep when you can. One of the first things she'd learned as a Hawkeye recruit. Calls for action never arrived when expected. Or convenient. More than once, she'd been up more than twenty-four hours with no food and limited water.

As if on cue, her stomach growled. The protein bar she'd eaten before her workout had long since been metabolized. Logic told her not to be stubborn. After all, she was going to share a majority of her meals with Torin for the foreseeable future.

"Come on, Araceli. I won't bite." His grin was quick and lethal.

Damn him. Part of her wished he would. It might help get rid of the tension crawling through her so she could move on, forget him. There was no way any man could be as hot as she believed he would be.

"We'll go as coworkers. I promise, no critiques."

"Okay. Fine." She exhaled. "Give me half an hour to get settled." Mira grabbed her belongings and escaped to the back bedroom.

It took her each one of those thirty minutes to regain her composure.

When she rejoined him, he was at the kitchen table, doing something on his computer. "Ready?" he asked, pushing back.

"Yes." It was a total lie, and her half smile was a total fake.

He drove them to the French Quarter in his gloss-white SUV, and he handled traffic without getting frustrated, making her wonder if he ever betrayed ordinary human emotion.

"You don't like me," she said, wanting to get it out of the way.

"Like you?" He slid her a quick glance. "Never thought about it."

She sank a little in her leather seat. This was another time that maybe she should have kept her mouth shut.

"But respect you? Very much. I think you have a lot of talent."

"You were damn tough on me."

He didn't respond.

"In training." It had bothered her. Other recruits didn't receive as much of his attention as she did. It had been difficult not to take it personally.

"You scare me."

She blinked, then stared at him.

"You're a good agent. Great instincts."

"But...?" Mira raked her hair back from her forehead. Why was she doing this to herself?

"You're a maverick. As if you've got something to prove." He was silent for so long, she wondered if he was going to say anything more. "You remind me of someone." He shrugged. "She got herself killed."

Breath rushed out of her lungs. "I'm cautious."

He checked the mirrors before looking at her again. "So was she. And I still fucking buried her."

Though she squirmed beneath the intensity in his gaze, she defended herself. "I'm me, Commander. Don't confuse me with anyone else."

He lifted a shoulder but returned his attention to the road.

Agreeing to go out with him had been stupid. They weren't ordinary coworkers. He was still the trainer who found her lacking.

Maybe what bothered her was that he was at least partially right. She did have something to prove. Her father's voice was always in her head, whispering that she wasn't good enough, that she'd never measure up.

That Torin had seen her determination to prove her dad wrong scared the hell out of her.

She leaned back against the headrest. This assignment promised to be challenging and grueling, maybe the worst of her career.

Two weeks later

TOGETHER, MIRA AND TORIN EXITED THE VEHICLE PROVIDED by Hawkeye Security, then checked the surroundings as they walked around to the back of the Maison Sterling hotel.

Passersby continued down the sidewalk, most likely unaware that the door was used only by VIPs and a handful of residents of the exclusive building. "I'll let Barstow know we're in position."

Torin nodded, then walked away to check the rest of the perimeter.

After their uncomfortable discussion on the first night, he'd treated her as a trusted partner. They'd worked together well, and they swapped out the lead position, based on what seemed best for the situation at hand. When she was in charge, he never second-guessed her judgment.

The only unfortunate thing was that it was a slow time of the year, which meant they had too much downtime together. He'd been closemouthed about his personal life, avoiding her questions about family and friends. If he ever made personal calls, she was unaware of them. She and her best friend, Hallie, had gone out for happy hour a couple of times, but as far as Mira knew, he hadn't gotten together with anyone.

What he did do was exercise, a lot...to the point of exhaustion. He ran every morning. And he swam lap after lap while wearing a stupidly tight, stupidly small black swimsuit. Most men wore trunks, but not Torin. The constant sight of his tanned, ripped body rocketed her hormones into overdrive. Work and hitting the gym herself were the only distractions she had.

She dialed the phone, and when the team leader answered, she said, "Araceli and Carter are onsite."

"Guessing another half hour?" Barstow replied. "They're waiting for another bottle of tequila to be delivered."

"Roger that." Not a surprise. Celebrity protection came with a lot of delays.

"I'll keep you posted," Barstow promised.

She ended the call and pocketed the phone. "Approximately another thirty minutes," she told Torin when he returned.

Tonight's assignment was backing up the security team for The Crush, a mega-artist. Recognized as one of the biggest mainstream hip-hop artists in the country, he'd recently won a major music award. Because of his popularity, he had numerous endorsements, and had just finished an acting gig on a hit television show. As far as fame profiles went, this man was at the pinnacle.

Right now, he was taking a week off from his three-month-long tour and had decided to spend a night in the French Quarter before catching a flight to the Caribbean. As charismatic as he was generous and gregarious, The Crush wanted to please his fans. As a result, he signed lots of autographs and posed for pictures. When he went out, he sometimes posted his whereabouts on social media. Which meant protecting him was a security headache.

This evening, he had late dinner reservations and planned to take in some live music afterward. Since it was a Friday night, the crowds were going to be thick and boisterous. "But I'm guessing it's going to be closer to an hour."

"I wouldn't bet against you," Torin replied.

Despite the fact that it was only the end of April, the Southern air was thick and clammy. She'd already been in her bed reading when the call for backup came in.

Mira had opted for slacks and boots, along with a light blue button-down shirt. Since she didn't know what to expect tonight, she'd pulled on a blazer that would hold her phone and her stun gun, cleverly disguised as a lipstick container. Though discreet, its four million watts were surprisingly effective.

A droplet of moisture arrowed down her neck, and she lifted her ponytail for a moment.

"We've got plenty of time. You might as well head inside. Find some air-conditioning," Torin suggested.

Not a bad idea. "I'll stay close."

While Torin remained at his post, she wandered to the front of the hotel. Before entering, she glanced up at the historic brick building with its wrought-iron accents. It didn't take much effort to spot The Crush and several members of his group on a balcony. He held a glass, raised. As usual, he wore a fedora set at a jaunty angle. His white shirt—stark against his ebony skin—was held together by only the bottom two buttons. Maybe it was a trick of the light, but she was certain there was a shine on his muscular, shaved chest.

She pushed through the enormous revolving glass door, then stepped into the old-world—and blessedly cool—elegance of the Maison Sterling.

The front desk had no line, and a few couples were seated in leather chairs, sipping drinks.

An actual bar was farther in, and she walked toward it. Maybe it would be a unique destination on her next happy hour outing with Hallie. Mira scanned the posted menu, looking for her favorite, a hurricane. Of course, the Maison had its own version of the quintessential New Orleans drink. It was called the Cat Five, and featured five different kinds of rum instead of the traditional two. She loved the fruity cocktail, but this one was more than twice the price that she usually paid.

Of course, her favorite haunts didn't cater to Hollywood A-listers, musicians, politicians, or members of a rumored secret society.

"Would you like a table, ma'am?" the hostess asked.

She wished she could take a seat at the bar and enjoy the rest of the evening. Instead, Mira shook her head. "Thanks. No." Now that she'd cooled off, she exited into the wet, blanket-like atmosphere. Somehow, it was worse now than it had been.

The Crush was throwing Mardi Gras beads to a small crowd of women who'd gathered on the street.

She strode back to the valet stand. "You need to get the people onto the sidewalk."

"Losing battle."

No doubt. "Doesn't mean it's okay to ignore it." She walked back inside, to the front desk, then rapped her knuckles on the polished wood surface. "I need a manager."

When the man finally arrived, she glanced over her shoulder, indicating the front door. "Get those people out of here before someone gets hurt and you have a damn lawsuit on your hands."

"I'll handle it, ma'am."

Satisfied, but tossing a glare at the valet, she walked to the back of the building.

Of course, Torin was still in place, still as alert as he always was, seemingly impervious to the humidity or the distractions all around them. And as always, she had an all too feminine reaction to him.

Damn it all three ways to hell, why did he have to look so good?

Beneath a casual blazer, he wore his perennial black T-shirt. Because she'd seen him emerge from the bathroom last night after his shower wearing nothing more than a towel around his waist, she knew his muscular body was nicked by scars, some nicely healed, others that looked as if they'd never received attention. Unfortunately for her, they added to his mystique and the power he held over her.

After she went to bed, she'd had disturbing dreams, haunted by images of him—ordering her to her knees, fisting his hand in her hair as he forced her to look up at his darkly brooding face.

In one dream, he'd pinned her on the floor and yanked off

her pants as she'd screamed yes over and over again. She'd awakened, out of breath, shaking, heart racing. Overwhelmed, she'd tossed back the blankets, jumped out of bed, then spent twenty minutes on the exercise bike before standing beneath the shower's hot spray until the water heater had been drained. Still, it had taken another hour to fall asleep again.

When he met her gaze, the phantom memory returned, with a flame threatening to devour her.

She wasn't sure what, but she needed to do something to get this man out of her thoughts.

"All good?"

"He's tossing beads from the balcony." She shrugged. "I talked to a manager."

A car honked, and brakes squealed.

Biting out a curse, she grabbed her phone and called the Hawkeye team leader. "Shut him down," she instructed.

When Barstow agreed, she looked at Torin again. "It's going to be impossible to get The Crush out of the hotel without getting mobbed." Which was probably okay with him.

A couple of minutes later, a small group of women walked around the building to stand near them.

"What are you waiting for?" Mira asked.

"The Crush." A blonde in faded denim shorts that had strategic holes in them held her cell phone in front of her camera ready. "You're with him, right?" the blonde asked.

"Nah. Just hanging out," Torin replied easily, not moving away from the building.

"You're a bodyguard."

"We do this all the time," the tallest of the group added. "There will be a hundred people in the lobby, waiting, but he won't go through there. And they all have people who say the same thing you do."

"You got us, then." Torin smiled. "Could be a long wait. Don't know that he's planning to go out tonight."

"They all say that too," the blonde stated.

Clearly, the fan was an expert.

Local police arrived to usher fans off the streets and onto the sidewalks, and fortunately someone managed to get The Crush back inside his room. Even though an hour ticked past, the women at the back door never budged.

The blonde, however, reapplied her lipstick for the third time. Not believing her friend that it looked fine, she took a selfie to check for herself.

In her pocket, Mira's phone vibrated with a message. As she pulled out the device, Torin was also checking his.

THE PRINCIPAL'S ON THE MOVE.

A STRETCH LIMO, ONE MEANT TO ACCOMMODATE A PARTY OF twenty, double-parked near the exit, ignoring honking cars.

Though neither Torin nor Mira spoke, the blonde moved several feet closer to the exit. Mira sidled in, putting herself between the woman and the door.

Torin pushed away from the building.

"That means he's coming!" the brunette exclaimed.

Mira shrugged. Saying anything seemed pointless.

"Oh my God!" The blonde squealed. "He just posted a picture of himself standing near the elevator."

Almost all of the celebrities Mira worked with preferred to go out incognito. They donned ball caps and sunglasses and didn't broadcast their whereabouts.

This man, though, fed off the frenzy.

It promised to be a really long night.

Instead of emerging at a brisk pace like most protectees,

The Crush strolled out, flanked by his entourage, four Hawkeye agents, and what looked to be two of his own bodyguards.

When the blonde screamed out his name and shouted, "I love you!" he stopped and smiled.

"I'll die unless I get a picture with you."

"Sir," Barstow said to The Crush. "We should keep moving."

With an apologetic smile to Barstow, The Crush waved the woman over.

Grinning and chatting, he posed for half a dozen selfies, then a dozen more with the entire group of women.

When a few more spotted them and squealed and broke into a run toward them, Mira and Torin inserted themselves between him and the oncoming group and nodded toward Barstow.

"Let's move, now," Barstow said. "Not a suggestion, sir."

"Sorry, ladies." The Crush smiled and posed with his knees slightly bent and both thumbs up for a few seconds, waiting for the fans to take a few more shots. Then, with obvious reluctance, he allowed his entourage to move him along.

Mira and Torin stood side by side and took up as much room as they could to discourage the women from following.

"That's it!" Torin called when the limo eased away from the curb. "He's gone."

Because the first group of women were starstruck as they walked away from their encounter with The Crush, they provided a barrier to the other fans.

A second car arrived for her and Torin. By prearrangement, The Crush's driver circled the block while she and Torin ensured everything was prepared at the upscale restaurant on Bienville Street.

Inside, Mira took the lead, introducing herself to the maître d' to confirm the private dining room.

"Yes, ma'am," the woman said. "The Vieux Carré Room is prepared, on the upper landing. Last door on the left. You'll have exclusive use of the entire floor."

Torin lifted his index finger, indicating he was going to check it out.

When he returned, he nodded, and she called Barstow to confirm everything was good.

Torin positioned himself at the bottom of the curbed staircase, and she stationed herself midway between him and the restaurant's entrance.

Less than five minutes later, the limousine glided to a stop directly in front of the restaurant. A Hawkeye member was the first out, and he stood sentry while the passengers exited.

The transfer to the second story went without incident.

"Not so bad," she said to Torin as she closed the door behind her.

Without responding, he wandered the mezzanine area, glanced over the wrought-iron railing, then paced back again.

A short time later, a server exited the dining room carrying two paper cups on a silver tray. "Compliments of The Crush."

"What is it?" she asked.

"Café au lait."

No wonder the man was universally liked.

"Thank you." She accepted the gift and took a sip of the steaming chicory-flavored beverage. It was an unexpected and welcome treat when a short-term protectee remembered their bodyguards.

Torin raised his cup toward her. "The good news is, we have tomorrow night off."

She grinned. "I wouldn't count on that. If the coffee's any indication, we might still be on this assignment."

"This is one time I'm hoping you're wrong."

Dinner lasted much longer than their beverages. She bent over into a couple of yoga stretches not just to stay alert, but also to keep her body fluid in case she needed to act quickly.

Finally, closer to midnight than eleven, and after most of the other patrons had already left the restaurant, Barstow sent a message that the limousine was out front and that their car was behind it. The Crush's destination was Bourbon Street. She'd hoped he'd select Frenchmen's Street where the crowds were smaller and more sober and celebrities were passé, but she wasn't surprised by his pulse-pounding, frenetic choice.

She and Torin jogged down the stairs to prepare the way for their client, and they had him in the vehicle and underway in less than a minute.

They arrived at the Front Door, a live-music venue in a building that had served as a brothel in the late nineteenth century. Since they hadn't called ahead, she and Torin bypassed the line to grab the bouncer's attention. This guy was even bigger than Bear at the training center.

"We need to see a manager," Torin said.

"Don't got one."

"We need to make arrangements for a VIP," she added.

The guy rolled his eyes. No doubt he'd heard every line.

"A manager," she repeated.

He looked them over and scratched his beard. Obviously deciding they didn't look like partygoers, the guy hooked his thumb over his shoulder. "Talk to the owner. Tall dude. Hawaiian shirt. Might be playing with the band."

"Hey!" the man behind them called out. "We got a VIP in our party." Snickers accompanied the proclamation. "Can we get in too?"

As Torin pulled the door open, she blinked. Strobe lights spun and flashed, disorienting her. The thumping bass reverberated, spiking her anxiety. At least a hundred people were packed into the bar, and shot girls wove through the crowd, pouring alcohol down their throats as others cheered them on.

She spotted the owner and pointed him out to Torin.

Since he was only able to make out their general meaning, he ushered them into a tiny room with an uneven wooden desk and ladder-back chair. The walls were painted a deep old-blood red, and much of it had flaked or faded over the years.

Even with the door shut, Torin still had to shout to be heard.

"The Crush?" the manager echoed. "No shit? How many people you got?"

"About twenty."

"We can do that. Gonna take time. Assume you wanna bring him in the back door?"

Torin nodded.

"We got a three-drink minimum for the night."

"Guessing it won't be a problem," Mira assured him.

Once people were moved, tables were shoved together, and stools were rounded up from back rooms, The Crush arrived.

One woman's eyes widened, and she pulled a friend close and pointed. Though they giggled and took photos, they remained where they were.

After the group was settled, she and Torin split up. He stood near the back door in case they needed to extract their client, and she propped her shoulders against a wall next to the group. From her vantage point, Mira had a good view of the venue's occupants.

The entourage ordered a couple of bottles of the proprietor's finest spirits, and The Crush settled back to listen to the band.

During a set break, the owner came over to introduce himself.

"Mind if I sit in?" The Crush asked.

Shit. That meant he'd be on stage.

The man grinned. "Reckon it can be arranged."

Suddenly the evening had gotten a whole lot more challenging. She grabbed her phone to update Torin.

After a nudge from the barkeep, the band leader wandered over to shake hands, select a song, and confirm the timing.

When the details were set, she sent them to Torin. The third song would be "Your Love Forevermore," one of The Crush's top ten hits, and made popular on a movie soundtrack. It was midtempo, soulful and deep, ending in tragedy. He'd jump on the stage during the first chorus, finish out the track with the band, then run through the refrain an extra time at the end to leave the crowd on an upbeat note. After that, his bodyguards would escort him back to the table.

Which seemed an unlikely scenario to her. Fans would want autographs. He'd want to give them.

When it was time for The Crush to go on, she and Torin accompanied him to the stage. The moment the audience realized they had a star in their midst, the screams began. Almost everyone yanked out their cell phones to take snapshots, which meant the performance would be all over social media within minutes.

Two bodyguards from his personal team flanked the stairs, while a couple of the Hawkeye agents positioned themselves at the corners of the stage. She and Torin stood toward the front of the crowd, right in the middle, poised to move any direction.

Shot girls wiggled between the swaying, screaming people, adding to the mayhem.

As he reached the refrain, a woman began screaming and sobbing. Mira flicked a glance that direction, ensuring there was no threat from her near-hysterical reaction to being so close to The Crush. When the woman's friends consoled her, Mira continued scanning the attendees.

Midway through the song, a man rushed forward, shouting obscenities, screaming that The Crush had no talent.

Mira moved quick, inserting herself between him and the stage. "Step it down," she instructed.

"The fuck out of my way!"

"Back the hell up!" She flattened her palms on his chest and shoved him back. He was huge, immovable, reeking of alcohol, eyes wide, focused on The Crush and nothing else. Torin fought through the crowd toward her.

She leaned toward the heckler. "Last warning."

"I told you to get the fuck out of my way, bitch!"

From her jacket pocket, she pulled out her small stun gun.

Torin nodded.

The crazed man fisted his enormous hand. Before she could act, he clocked her upside of the head. Seeing stars, she swallowed hard and fought through the sudden nausea to press the tip of the stun gun against the asshole's upper hip. Her hand shook as she sought the green button.

On the first try, she missed it and accidentally activated the flashlight feature. But on the second attempt, four million volts surged into him. Even with his amped-up energy from booze and whatever else he was taking, the charge was enough for him to immediately start to shake, then for his limbs to weaken.

Torin was there, behind the guy to catch him.

Even though her head was still swimming, she grabbed his legs.

"The fuck, man?" one of his buddies demanded.

"Your friend appears drunk," Torin shouted as they carried him to a chair. "Maybe you should get him home."

"What the hell happened to him?"

"Passed out." Torin shrugged. "Good thing I was there to catch him. He should be more careful in the future."

The man opened his mouth to speak, and Torin guided her away. "You okay?"

"I doubt I'll even have a headache later." Which was a straight-out lie.

"You can sit out for a bit. Take a breather."

Oh hell no. "No need."

"Araceli, you got your bell rung. It's okay to admit—"

"I'm okay." She appreciated his concern, but she wouldn't let down any of her teammates. There was a job to do, a client to keep safe. "Really."

Mouth in a tight, disbelieving line, Torin nodded.

Together, they threaded their way back to the front, using a firm, no-nonsense tone.

Instead of heading back to his table after the song ended, The Crush conferred with the band's lead vocalist while the guitarist launched into a riff to keep the crowd occupied.

A few seconds later, the singer took the mic and announced another song with The Crush and signaled to his bandmates.

The audience was captivated by the haunting lyricism of a relationship gone bad. The Crush closed his eyes, as if giving himself over to emotional pain.

Over the years, she'd protected some well-regarded singers. But she'd never been swept away by their talent. This man bled through is voice. She was quickly becoming a fan.

When the song ended, the crowd launched into rapturous

applause, catcalls, screams. More people than was legal had shoved inside the door, and after they had him securely back with his entourage, Torin found the owner to tell him to get rid of some of the patrons before the fire department showed up.

She glanced toward the guy she'd stunned. Though he was still sitting, he was doing well enough to allow one of the shot girls to pour a blue-colored drink into his open mouth.

"I see our friend is okay," she observed when he rejoined her.

"Stupid runs deep."

It was close to four a.m. when the group called it a night.

"Breakfast?" Torin suggested as The Crush's limo's taillights faded from view.

Right now, adrenaline was keeping her upright. When it faded, she'd drop on her ass. If she ate now, hunger might not wake her up in a couple of hours.

"Shamrock Grill's a couple blocks down."

Her tummy rumbled.

"I'll take that as a yes." He grinned, easing tension from his features.

When his tone was teasing like that, he became even more irresistible, sneaking beneath her defenses.

They walked down Bourbon Street. Several bars were still open and had plenty of customers. It took some time in the relative quiet for her ears to stop ringing.

All the tables at the Shamrock were filled, so they seated themselves at the counter on red-vinyl-covered stools.

She opted for eggs and toast while Torin dug into a massive pork chop with mashed potatoes and fried okra.

After a drink of his black coffee, he pushed the cup aside. "Hell of a performer, isn't he? The Crush."

"I'd go see him in concert."

He reached forward to feather back her hair.

34

She froze, wide-eyed. Heat, long and slow, arced through her. She told herself to pull away. No other partner had ever touched her like that, and she shouldn't allow him to be the first. But her lips parted, and she remained where she was. "What are you doing?"

"Checking the swelling. That guy hit you pretty hard."

"I'm... It's fine."

"Not completely. You've got a bruise to go along with a nasty bump."

"I'll put some ice on it when we're back at the carriage house." But she wouldn't, mostly because it had been so many hours ago that she doubted treating it would do much good.

"Yeah." Slowly, he lowered his hand. "Good plan."

To him, the touch had been perfunctory. It meant nothing. But her pulse was thready. Ever since the beginning, she'd had disturbing reactions to Torin. Being with him was making her reactions more intense, not less.

Trying to ignore him—and failing—Mira concentrated on slathering raspberry jam on a piece of toast that she didn't really plan to eat.

Every bit of her was aware of him, his crisp scent, the shadow of beard on his strong chin. And when she hazarded a glance up, he was staring at her, his electric-blue eyes hooded and brooding. "What?" she asked.

"Nothing."

He drummed his fingers on the hilt of his knife, his body language saying otherwise. But he shifted his focus, to the almost empty coffee cup, making sure she could no longer see his whole face. "You going to keep all of your thoughts to yourself?"

"Not hiding anything."

"Right. You're a regular open book, Commander."

"Eat your toast, Araceli." He snatched up the bill, then strode to the cashier to pay. "I need to get you to bed."

CHAPTER TWO

HAWKEYE

"Going somewhere, Commander Carter?" Mira glanced up from the British crime drama she was streaming and muted the television. Just as he had for the past two Monday nights, Torin was leaving the carriage house around nine p.m. If his usual pattern held, he'd return sometime after one. It didn't matter to her where he went, but the fact that he didn't volunteer the information made her curious. And when she'd asked, he'd given a vague half answer, intriguing her further.

"Don't wait up," he responded.

Though they'd been under the same roof, sharing a bathroom, eating most meals together, partnering for over a dozen operations, they kept their private lives as protected as possible. She trained at the gym, met with Hallie for a couple of happy hours, indulged in the occasional café au lait, visited some of New Orleans's best galleries, and tried to ignore the effect her former instructor had on her sex drive.

Tonight, he was wearing a long-sleeved white dress shirt and tailored slacks. His shoes were polished to a high-shine. He smelled of temptation.

"Hot date?"

"Fishing for information?" he countered.

"Nah." Pretending disinterest, she turned the volume back up.

The moment the door sealed behind him, she moved to the window and nudged back the blinds to watch him reverse out of the garage. As if knowing she was there, he stopped near a lamppost and lifted his right index finger in acknowledgment.

Did he miss nothing?

As she'd already planned to, she crossed to the kitchen table, snagged her keys, then waited until the gate closed behind him before jogging down the stairs to her car.

A short time later, she was behind him on the road. Keeping a couple of vehicles between them, she followed him onto Saint Charles Avenue. When he turned onto Loyola, she raised her eyebrows. The French Quarter? Seemed likely since this was the same route he'd traveled when he took her to dinner that first night.

She lost him on a narrow pedestrian-and-vehicle-packed one-way street. Having no other real option, she continued on, then spotted him again entering a parking lot on Iberville. It wasn't the same one he'd used when they went to dinner. She pulled over, parking illegally next to the curb, waiting for him.

Eventually, he emerged to head down Royal Street. Last week, she'd browsed art galleries there, but she was guessing he wasn't interested in paintings or sculptures.

Knowing the risk of a ticket—or worse, getting towed—she slipped out of her car to follow him.

As if suspecting he had a tail, or just taking appropriate precautions, he darted through jammed, honking vehicles and turned onto Toulouse, heading deeper into the heart of the French Quarter.

As quick as she could, she followed him, down a couple of blocks until…

She pressed her back against a nearby building as he opened an unmarked green door. One she knew well. The Quarter, New Orleans's oldest, most vaunted BDSM club.

Holy hell.

Torin Carter was a Dom? And he attended *her* club?

She dragged in a deep breath. Her fantasies about him hadn't been far out of line. Had something deep inside her intuitively responded to his unspoken vibe?

A tourist carrying a camera jostled into her, dragging her back to reality.

Still hardly able to think, she pushed away from the wall and joined the throngs on the sidewalk.

Now what? Even if it meant seeing him there, Mira refused to give up her occasional visit. BDSM scenes weren't just something casual for her. They were much more than a simple, pleasurable release. Inside the construct and rules, she could be free, let go in ways she wasn't able to in the outside world. Participating fed something essential inside her.

In front of her, a reveler lurched to a stop, and she bumped into him. "Sorry." She shook her head as a way to forcibly reel in her thoughts. Allowing Torin's secret and its implications to distract her was a sure way to lose her edge.

Focusing on where she was going, she walked to a corner restaurant and ordered a muffuletta sandwich to go. It was ginormous enough to feed her for two meals.

When she returned to her car, there was a parking ticket on it. *Of course.* At least she hadn't been towed.

The later it got, the more difficult it became to navigate the narrow one-way streets. Many pedestrians didn't even look before stepping into traffic.

The drive back to the mansion took much longer than the

trip to the French Quarter, and her mind was still scattered when she parked on the property.

Because safety was ingrained, she checked the grounds before entering the carriage house and closing the door behind her.

On automatic, she ate part of her sandwich, then wrapped the remainder and stored it in the refrigerator. Restless, she checked email. Still empty. And no notifications on social media. That wasn't a surprise. Because of the nature of her job, she rarely posted her whereabouts or anything personal. She glanced at the latest memes from her friends. A lot of them had to do with parenting or whether it was wine o'clock yet.

It was as if everyone she knew had a totally different experience of being alive than she did.

Mira closed her browser and plopped onto the couch in front of the television to scroll through the programming guide. There were at least a hundred choices, and none of them captured her interest.

With a sigh, she admitted the truth to herself.

She wanted to go to the club.

Action was the only thing that soothed her and allowed her to put her demons to rest.

Mira stood, turned off the television, then picked up her phone to call Hallie. "Are you still planning to go to the Quarter Wednesday night?"

"Oh my God." Silence echoed between them. "Are you serious? Tell me you're coming!"

She and Hallie had attended the same boarding school, then later, college. Even though they couldn't be more different, they'd roomed together and become lifelong friends.

"Earth to Mira."

"Sorry." She shook her head. "Yes…or, well…I'm thinking about it."

"That will make it so much more fun!"

"I'll be on duty, so there's a chance I'll get a last-minute assignment." Since it was a Wednesday night and the schedule was still clear, things looked good.

"It's a Victorian theme night. You have something to wear, right?"

"No."

"Even better! Let's meet tomorrow at the costume store, then go to happy hour at the Maison Sterling. Ever since you mentioned it, I've wanted to try it. Four o'clock?"

After they ended call, Mira turned the television on again. The drama couldn't hold her attention, and neither could a stand-up comedian.

An hour later, she gave up again, she changed into her bathing suit and headed down the stairs to the hot tub.

She sank into the water up to her neck, then tipped her head back and closed her eyes.

Where was Torin now? Sitting in the bar, observing what was happening in the main dungeon? Scening with some lucky sub?

Damnation and fuck it all.

She didn't want to allow her thoughts to go there.

Did he have someone? A sub? If he had a girlfriend, he wouldn't have been able to hide it for the month they'd been assigned together. But it was completely possible for him to have a woman he played with at the Quarter.

Taunted by her own thoughts, she left the tub in favor of making a few laps in the swimming pool.

The water was blessedly cool on her skin, and the within a few minutes, she was able to banish thoughts of him pleasing some unnamed woman…at least until she went to bed to toss and turn.

Around two, she woke up, dragged out of a deep sleep.

She climbed out of bed and grabbed her robe. As she left the bedroom, she tightened the belt.

The front door was closed and locked. Torin's bedroom door stood ajar, and there was no sign of him anywhere in the carriage house. His wallet wasn't on the counter, and the jacket he'd been wearing wasn't hanging from the peg near the door. Obviously, he hadn't returned from his night out.

Without turning on any lights, she walked to a window. The courtyard was empty, and trees swayed in the gentle breeze.

She wandered toward a window on the far side of the carriage house for a different view when a key turned in the lock.

Moments later, Torin entered and flipped on a light switch.

He stood there, completely naked, holding his clothes.

Water droplets shimmered on his smooth, bare chest, and his dick—*massive dick,* some wild part of her thoughts corrected—was pulsingly erect.

She ordered herself to look away, perhaps mumble something as she fled. Instead, she was immobilized.

"Sorry if I disturbed you."

Being a light sleeper was a hazard of the job.

Torin offered no apology for his nakedness, and in fact, seemed completely unconcerned about it.

Of course, she'd seen him in his swimwear and from a distance. This, though, was different. His muscles were clearly delineated, and if she reached out, she could skim her fingers over his taut, gorgeous muscles.

He turned to close the door, giving her a full view of his tight ass. This was the perfect opportunity for her to excuse herself, but instead, she stood where she was, unmoving.

He placed his clothes on a nearby table, then, in silence, faced her again. His cock was scant inches from her.

"You should go back to bed."

He'd given voice to her thoughts. But his prompting didn't make her walk away.

"Final warning, Araceli."

"Or what?" Her words were a whisper, more of an invitation than a challenge.

"Or what?" He swirled his hand into her hair. "I'm going to kiss you."

No. *Yes.*

Smelling of sin and danger, he leaned in, bringing his magnificently erect cock even closer to her. "Tell me not to."

This, inviting him, tempting him, was foolish. He might be able to fuck her and forget her, move on with his life. But to her, it would mean something, no matter how much she tried to pretend it wouldn't. And yet… Even if she might get hurt, she wanted him. "I might die if you don't."

He brushed his lips across hers in a sweet, tender gesture that was completely unexpected. He'd been at the Quarter, so she'd anticipated he would claim her in a much more dominant manner.

Then she recognized his strategic brilliance. The brief touch fed her hunger, rather than sated it. "Carter…"

"You're so fucking desirable, Mira."

At the use of her first name, with a slight, sexy roll to *r*, her tummy fluttered. She reached up to loop her arms around his neck. His skin was cool and damp, and droplets from his hair dripped onto her forearm.

"That's it." He captured her chin. "Give me what I want."

Responding to him, she lifted onto her toes. Except for that night in training, they'd never been this close. The reality was more overwhelming than she remembered.

She kissed him, then captured his lower lip with her teeth. He groaned, turning her on. The moment she released him, she soothed the tiny bite with a soft kiss.

"You read me right, Araceli."

His approval made her pulse skitter.

"And now…" He seized control, blue eyes darkening with intent.

This time, he sought entrance to her mouth, and she yielded, opening wide for him. He tasted faintly of whiskey. Bourbon, maybe. If so, that meant he hadn't scened at the club, unless he'd headed for the bar after a very brief encounter. That, she couldn't imagine.

He moved a hand to the center of her back and placed the other at the curve of her spine. It was intimate, and yet…not, as if he was holding part of himself back.

With restrained power, he brought her in a little closer. His cock pressed against her, making the world swirl. He deepened the kiss, exploring her responses, finding what she liked and giving her more of that.

Mira met his slow, sensual dance and surrendered to it until she went dizzy. Her body softened, and she tightened her grip on him so that she could remain upright.

For a moment, he ended the kiss, giving her time to inhale a shaky breath. But he never let go. In fact, he spread his fingers farther apart so he could hold her more completely.

"I'm not done with you."

"Good."

With a deep sound of approval, he claimed her again.

This time, he wasn't gentle. He thrust his tongue into her mouth possessively. She liked it every bit as much as the first kiss, and maybe even more.

He consumed her, igniting a flame that had been dormant for more than a year. Since she was focused on her career, she didn't indulge in casual sex. Suddenly, though, she ached, wanting to be filled, to be taken. But not by any man. By Torin.

She moved one of her arms and dug her fingers into his hair.

Slowly, he eased back.

Part of her was grateful, another, not at all.

When he lowered his hands, she unwrapped herself from around him.

She met his gaze and was consumed by the way he looked at her. Longing. And… Regret? "I should go to bed," she said, an echo of his earlier sentiment.

"Agreed."

She took a step back. Her nightclothes were damp from his skin, and a couple of droplets of water clung to her. His turgid cock was pointed her direction, throbbing. Her hand trembled, and she wanted to reach out and explore him. Would he let her?

The answer didn't matter.

She was too smart to find out.

Mira hurried back to her room. She didn't care if she appeared to be fleeing. She was.

She shut the door with a decisive click, more for his benefit than hers.

In the dark, beneath the sheet, she pressed a hand against her swollen lips, reliving his tenderness as well as his urgency.

Whatever it was she felt for him, it disturbed her. She wanted to name it lust, but it was much deeper. Desire? Not deep enough. It was more like recognition. Inevitability. He saw into her, guessed her secrets, and he still wanted her.

She yanked the sheets around her shoulders, like a cocoon.

Torin Carter was a threat to her, not just because of her attraction, but because he had ghosts of his own, ones that weren't at rest.

In the bathroom, the water ran. She envisioned him beneath the spray, soaping his erection.

Moaning, she turned on her side. But she couldn't escape her imagination.

Knowing she'd never get to sleep, she reached for the tiny vibrator tucked beneath a paperback.

She worked her hand inside her panties. Then, with her eyes closed, the sounds from across the hall and the scent of clean, masculine soap on the air, she turned on the toy and pressed the tip against her clit.

Pressing her lips together so she didn't cry out, she nudged the power a little higher.

Then, lost, she moaned as an orgasm built.

Her thoughts ran wild, and she pictured Torin fastening her to a Saint Andrew's cross, or better, taking her upstairs to a private room at the Quarter where he could strip her completely bare. He'd use a flogger on her, one that had long, thick falls that would wrap around her, delivering dozens of simultaneous thuds to sear her nerve endings. He was a fit, powerful man, capable of the force she needed to achieve subspace.

Rationally, she knew she should fantasize about a nameless, faceless Dom, but Torin filled her senses.

So lost beneath his dominance, she screamed out as she orgasmed.

Out of breath, she dropped the still-humming vibrator and dragged in a dozen desperate breaths.

As reality returned, she became aware of a preternatural quiet.

The water was no longer running. The air conditioner was silent.

Seconds later, a footfall echoed outside her room. Shortly thereafter, his bedroom door closed.

Torin had been there? Listening?

Embarrassed, praying she hadn't called out his name, she turned off the vibrator. How the hell would she face him in the morning?

The remaining weeks loomed larger than ever. And she was less and less certain about her ability to survive.

———

"ARE YOU KIDDING ME?" HALLIE DEMANDED AS SHE FASTENED the top button of Mira's Victorian gown.

In the dressing room mirror, she met her friend's gaze. As Hallie had helped her into the long red gown, Mira recounted last night's events with Torin.

"So you're sure he was outside your door while you were, ah, polishing your pearl?"

"I'm sure of it."

"Well, at least he didn't walk in on you."

"He's my partner. I would have died for real, if he had."

"You have nothing to be embarrassed about. What the hell could he have expected after he kissed you and flashed you his full-staff dick?"

Because of Hallie's support, Mira was able to laugh.

"He was probably patting himself on the back."

Maybe.

"I bet he beat off in the shower."

"Hallie!"

"Girl, if he wasn't proud of that thing, he wouldn't have walked around in all his naked glory."

Mira didn't point out that he'd probably believed she was asleep.

"What do you think of the dress?"

Mira studied her reflection. "It's a little tight across the chest." But the waist was perfect. "I like it."

"Do you have shoes you can wear?"

She hadn't thought about that. "No."

"I have some you can borrow. Come by around nine, and then we can take a car from my place." Hallie went on for a few more minutes before winding down. "We're going to have fun. You can find someone to take your mind off Mr. Hard Dick."

With a grin, Mira shook her head.

After she changed back into her boring work clothes and paid the rental fee, she hung up the dress in her car. She and Hallie left their vehicles in the lot and caught a taxi to the Maison Sterling.

"Damn," Hallie said as they walked beneath the green awning.

The door was opened by a man dressed in livery, who tipped his top hat as they entered.

"I've driven past, and I knew it was nice, but..." Obviously at a loss for words, she repeated, "Damn."

"My reaction as well." Mira's boots echoed off the polished marble floor.

They found tall stools at the elegant bar. Within moments, the bartender appeared, with a crystal bowl filled with nuts.

"Oh my God." Hallie picked out a cashew. "These are primo. Not even a single peanut among them. Be still my heart!"

Even though the hurricane was outrageously priced, Mira decided to splurge. After all, there was no way she could drink more than one.

Hallie selected the happy hour house wine. It was still more money than almost anywhere else in town, but the ambience was first rate. Lights were dimmed. Candles sat atop each table. Light jazz played, softly enough that it didn't drown out conversation. The chairs appeared to be hand carved, and the others throughout the area were real leather.

At a table across the room, a couple was cozying up, so into each other that they didn't appear to even notice anyone else. At another, away from anyone, their backs at a slight angle to hide their faces, two men conferred over highball glasses.

"Can you ever give the spy stuff a rest?"

"I'm in protection. That's totally different than being a spy," Mira protested.

Hallie rolled her eyes. "Don't tell me you haven't noticed every single detail of what's going on here."

She gave a half smile. Being a good agent meant she needed to be aware of her surroundings. Her life, and that of her principal, might depend on it.

"That couple…" Hallie prompted.

"An affair. She's cheating on her husband."

Hallie frowned.

"Her diamond flashed when she put her left hand on his shoulder."

"They could be on their honeymoon."

"Not with the way she checks her phone." Mira plucked the cherry from her drink and sucked on it before biting into the delicious sweetness. "Those men over there…" She inclined her head. "One's got money. The other's a politician."

"Cash for influence?"

The way of the world.

"I don't care what you say," Hallie proclaimed. "Figuring out all that stuff is spy shit."

"No. It's just a casual observation."

Hallie shook her head. "Not true. I observed two guys having a drink."

"They're in the far corner, away from the other patrons. No one walking through the lobby can see that part of the bar. Oh. And. They moved their candle to another table."

"See?" Hallie demanded. "Freaking spy shit!" She took a drink. "Where as me, a mere mortal, have just *observed* a prime specimen of masculine glory."

Mira glanced over her shoulder. Hallie was definitely right. The gentleman striding confidently across the floor was exceptionally handsome.

"Evening Mr. Sterling," the bartender greeted.

When the tall, striking man was out of earshot, Hallie signaled for the bartender to come over. "Is that him? The owner? Like *the* Mr. Sterling. As in Sterling Hotels?"

"It is."

"Wow."

He pulled up a chair to join the other two men.

"Worth the cost of the wine to sit here and people watch," Hallie observed.

It was. After a few sips of the Cat Five hurricane, Mira pushed the glass aside and ordered a sparkling water. "It's lethal," she told the bartender.

The woman grinned. "There's a reason we list a warning on the menu."

Mira leaned toward Hallie. "Now it's your turn. Tell me what's going on with you."

Hallie fished out a few more nuts before sighing. "What makes you think there's anything?"

"Seriously?" Mira raised eyebrow. "Do-or-die friends know these things."

"Uh-huh."

Mira grinned. "Okay, you've got a tell, like a poker player might. You've said almost nothing the whole time we've been together. You're keeping the conversation all about me and my life, which means you're being evasive. And you avoided my question just this minute. Ergo..." She paused for dramatic effect. "There's something you don't want to tell me"

"That's spy shit," Hallie protested, looking down at her glass.

"And… There you go again. Start talking. Otherwise the interrogation begins. I might even get out the thumbscrews."

Hallie shook her head. "You would, too."

"Waiting."

Hallie pushed away her wineglass. "So I met a guy."

"Oh?"

"And no, you can't have his full name, and I do not want you to run a background check on him."

Mira remembered, all too well, what happened the last time Hallie had been so secretive. Her anguish, the tears, the hospital visit… Mira put her hand over her friend's. "Hal—"

"If it gets serious, then you can." She pulled away her hand with an exhalation. "This time, I'm smarter. I promise."

Having no other choice, Mira nodded. "I care about you."

"I appreciate it. But I want to find out more on my own. I mean, assuming it goes anywhere."

As she waited, Mira took a sip of her water.

"I met him at the Quarter."

That helped, just a little. The club owner, Mistress Aviana, vetted all members. But she relied on referrals more than extensive background checks.

"He visits periodically. Lives in Baton Rouge."

It was a commute, for sure, but doable.

"We've played twice, and after the last time, we had a drink before he took me home."

"And…?" She took the lime from the rim of her glass and placed it on the napkin.

"He's…" Hallie paused. "Nice."

Mira hated being a skeptic, but she was. Maybe because she'd rarely met nice men. It didn't mean they didn't exist, but in her world, they didn't. "Give me a first name, at least."

"Master Bartholomew."

"A scene name?" she guessed. Plenty of people used them, herself included. Since she didn't want anyone finding her outside of the club, she went by Ember when she was there, and she never shared her phone number or surname. To her, when she was at the club, she was able to be someone else, and she liked the freedom it gave her.

Hallie looked into her glass.

"You don't know for sure." She swallowed back a sigh. Shit. Even though she protected her identity, she would reveal parts of herself if she were interested in someone. That he hadn't done that much concerned her. "He took you home?"

Hallie nodded. "He walked me to the door, like a perfect gentleman."

"And then what?"

"Nothing." She plucked a cashew from the dish, but she didn't eat it. "He kissed my hand and said good night."

"When was that?"

"Last week."

"And you haven't heard from him since?"

"A text message last night. He'll be out of town for a week."

Hurt wove through Hallie's words, making Mira cringe. "But the scenes were good?"

"He was thoughtful, and…" She smiled, vanquishing her former gloom. "Yes. They've been epic."

"Epic? Then concentrate on that."

"I will." Hallie finally popped the nut into her mouth. "It's better than thinking about work. It still sucks. Too damn many unfilled positions. Always trying to do more with less. Any openings at Hawkeye for math geeks like me?"

Hallie was an office manager at an oil and gas firm that was cycling through another downturn. "You should apply,"

Mira encouraged. "Use my name. Or better, let me call HR and recommend you."

"I'll think about it. Vacation time, retirement..."

The realities of leaving a job.

They finished their drinks, and she watched the politician leave the table. A few minutes later, Mr. Sterling followed suit. The businessman lingered, typing lots of notes into his phone before pocketing the device and adjusting his blazer. After checking his watch, he strode from the bar.

"All that power in one place," Hallie said. "We have to come back here again."

"It definitely is a good place to people watch," Mira agreed before relating the story of protecting The Crush.

"Okay, that's it. I'm applying at Hawkeye."

Mira laughed. "I promise, it's not nearly as glamorous as it sounds."

"But you hung out with The Crush."

"I was about as close to him as we were to that politician. And I got a black eye from the overzealous fan who wanted to climb onto the stage."

The man who'd been snuggled up to the woman stood. Then he left, with a couple of sad over-the-shoulder glances.

After refreshing her lipstick, the woman signaled for a server to clear the table, then ordered a glass of white wine.

A few minutes later, another man—presumably her husband this time—joined her.

"You called that one right," Hallie observed, finishing the last of her drink.

Since she had to drive, Mira gave up on the hurricane. "Next time, I'll catch a ride from the house so I can drink the whole thing."

After finalizing the plans for meeting at the Quarter the next evening, they exited. A valet flagged down a cab to take them back to the costume store.

From there, the drive back to the carriage house took less than fifteen minutes.

She grabbed her purse and the costume from the car and wasn't sure whether or not to be relieved when she discovered Torin wasn't in the pool. She didn't have to worry about seeing his naked body, but it also meant he was probably inside where she couldn't avoid him.

He was cycling on the exercise bike when she entered. Thankfully, he was wearing a shirt and shorts. She was starting to fear that spontaneous combustion might be a real thing.

"Need a hand?"

"Thanks. I've got it all." She placed her purse on the counter, then locked the door.

"What have you got?" he asked.

She debated her answer, then stuck to the truth. No doubt he'd noticed the name on the garment bag. "It's a Victorian gown. For an event tomorrow night."

"Ah."

Mira carried the gown down the hall and hung it in her closet. When she returned to the living area, he had a towel draped around his neck, and he'd opened an amber ale from the famous local brewery.

"Can I get you one?"

"Uh. No. I just had a Cat Five hurricane at the Maison Sterling."

"Sounds dangerous."

"It was slightly worse than that. I didn't finish the whole thing."

"How about a pizza?"

That had fast become a once-a-week tradition. "Sounds good." And normal.

"The usual?"

Mira nodded, relieved he was acting as if he hadn't kissed

her or stood outside her door while she moaned and maybe called out his name.

Forty minutes later, the open pizza box on the coffee table, he sat on the couch and turned on the television to an Australian drama about a lawyer who was currently in trouble with the tax collector. She selected a large slice of the double pepperoni, then curled up on a lounge chair.

He raised an eyebrow at her choice but said nothing.

After watching two back-to-back episodes that she'd paid almost no attention to, she stood. "Good night. I'm going to bed to read for a while,"

"Already?"

It wasn't even ten. "The aftereffects of the rum," she lied.

He watched her go.

When she reached the end of the hall, he called out, "Araceli."

The soft command in his voice stopped her cold. But she didn't look back at him.

"It happened. All of it. And at some point we're going to stop pretending it didn't and figure out what the hell to do with it."

She was fine with continuing as they were. "Taking it any further would be a mistake."

"One you want to make."

Then she did look back and wished she hadn't. He was so damn handsome, so inviting. Tempting.

The fact that he was right made it worse. "Good night, Commander Carter."

"So that's how it is."

She escaped into the bedroom and closed the door.

The book couldn't hold her interest. When the door to the outside closed with a slight *click*, she moved to the window. As she guessed, he was swimming, and there was no doubt he was naked.

Quickly, she dropped the blinds, determined not to let him, his statement—or his sexy body—get to her.

It took hours to harness her thoughts, and she didn't manage to fall asleep until he was back inside and out of the shower.

For another hour, she tossed and turned, drifting in and out of sleep, looking at the clock every ten minutes or so.

Around three, she awakened hard, alert.

"No!"

Torin?

"Goddamn it! Noooo!" Pain ripped through the word. "Noooo!"

She tossed back the sheet, then jumped out of bed to dash down the hall. She pounded on his closed door. "Commander Carter?" When there was no response, she turned the knob. "I'm fucking coming in!"

CHAPTER THREE

HAWKEYE

I n the darkness, broken only by ambient light from outside, she took in the scene. Wearing only a pair of boxer briefs, Torin was thrashing on the bed, the sheet tangled around his ankles. "Commander Carter!" She took a step into the room, then another. "Torin."

When he didn't respond, she sat on the edge of the mattress, near him, but far enough away that she could stand get away if he reacted badly. "Torin. Wake up!" She gently shook his shoulder.

He opened his eyes in a wide, unseeing stare.

"It's okay," she said, the words instinctive rather than genuine. She had no idea what the hell was going on, other than a nightmare…or closer to a terror. Whatever it was, he was deep in its horrid grips.

Mira reached out again, placing a reassuring hand on his heated skin. "You're safe."

Torin balled his hands at his sides.

"You're in the carriage house. New Orleans."

After a ragged exhalation, he blinked. Then, after a few

steadying breaths, he struggled out of the sheet and worked himself up onto his elbows.

Now that he was awake, she eased her hand back. She'd known he kept secrets, but she'd had no idea they were so destructive.

"Everything's fine," he said.

"I…" She shook her head. "Want to talk about it?"

He sat the rest of the way up. His breathing had returned to normal, and his steely eyes were focused. But the sheen was still on his skin, and his hair was wildly mussed.

"Everything's fine," he repeated, as if on automatic.

"No. It's not." She hated to think about him being alone when this happened, with no one around to anchor him to reality. "Have you seen someone about it?"

"Listen, Araceli…" He captured her wrist, not tightly, but in a loose circle. Then, studying his action, he feathered his thumb across her pulse point. "You never have bad dreams?"

"Of course." She should pull away from him. Instead, she, too, looked down, mesmerized by his long, gentle strokes, in contrast to his raw strength. After what had just happened, she appreciated the reassurance of their connection.

When he stilled, she glanced up to find him staring at her.

"That was beyond a bad dream."

"It's over now. You did your good deed."

"But—"

"Go back to your own room now, Araceli."

He was back to being himself, and he'd made it abundantly clear that staying wasn't an option.

In his place, she wouldn't want anyone to glimpse her vulnerabilities. She had to respect that, even if she didn't like it. She had questions that needed answers.

With a sigh, she stood. "Commander…"

"Thank you, Araceli."

On the threshold, she stopped.

"Close the door on your way out."

"You can be a total jerk, Carter." To see if her words stung, she glanced back.

Shocking her, he was smiling. There was nothing charming about it. Rather, it was feral, sending a deep shiver through her.

"Believe me, Araceli, you don't want me to invite you into my bed."

Oh God. *Jesus.* That was exactly what she wanted.

"I wouldn't be responsible for my actions."

He'd meant to warn her, no doubt. But her reaction was immediate. Sexual hunger crashed into her. Torin was a flame, and she yearned to touch it.

"I appreciate you coming to my rescue. Sleep well."

Remembering his torment, all mixed up with her craving to be with him, she was unable to settle.

Eventually she tossed back the covers and climbed out of bed to bend into a long yoga stretch that did nothing to center her.

She headed for the living room and the exercise bike, needing a grueling aerobic workout to exhaust her.

Torin Carter was troubled, far more than she'd realized.

She wanted to know why, even if he didn't want to tell her.

MIRA'S HEELS CLICKED ON THE CARRIAGE HOUSE'S HARDWOOD floor, little stabby points of sexy noise. Torin glanced up from his computer.

His eyes widened.

She wore a long gown, bloodred and stunning.

"What do you think?" Without waiting for his response,

she twirled, so slow that he had the opportunity to admire her from every angle.

Her long black hair—alive with flamelike highlights—was pinned back, and a few tendrils had escaped their delicate confines to curl alluringly across her cheeks and at her nape.

Belatedly, he recalled her saying she'd rented a gown. This one was cut fairly low, in a way he was pretty damn sure would have been scandalous when Queen Victoria sat on the British throne. The style of the dress emphasized the alluring swell of Mira's breasts.

Enticing vixen. "Going somewhere?"

"Don't wait up." She checked her phone, presumably to verify the arrival of her ride, then lifted her hand on the way out the door.

The fact that she repeated his words from earlier this week was a barb, and it found its mark.

He drummed his fingers on the table, wondering where the hell she was going. No wonder she followed him the other night. Because of their personality, no mystery remained unsolved.

Where was she going at nine o'clock on a Wednesday evening?

Doesn't matter. Or at least that was what he reminded himself. There were no ties between them. Soon enough, they'd go their separate ways. Perhaps their paths would never cross again.

That thought clouded his brain, getting in the way of rational thought.

Araceli meant something to him. Pure male lust, no doubt. But a whole sweet fuck more. She was fearless. That bothered him as much as the glimpses of her sweet, caring nature.

Last night, she should have tried to wake him from the far side of the room, if at all. Instead, she'd sat on the bed, touched him, despite the fact that she hadn't known what to expect.

Hell, *he* hadn't known what to expect.

It'd been over a year since his last episode. He'd thought, believed, they'd gone away.

He'd seen a shrink after Ekaterina had died on his watch. Talking about it had helped, at least enough for him to sleep four hours at a stretch. Still, on rare occasions, something would happen to trigger the memories.

No doubt, it was Araceli herself.

She worried him.

The fearlessness that he admired was the thing that scared him the most, as it had since she stepped foot into his classroom.

Restless, he headed outside for a swim.

When he was worn out, no longer obsessing over her, he headed back inside to shower.

The scent of wildflowers lingered on the air, exceptional because she generally didn't use anything more than an ordinary soap.

When he exited the shower, he noticed her garment bag, hanging from a hook on the back of the door.

With a towel wrapped around his waist, he read the inscription. Masquerade Costume Shop. *Original.* Then he plucked the receipt from the small plastic window on the front of the bag.

Victorian dress. Seventy-nine dollars.

More intrigued than ever, he strode back to the living room, powered up his computer, then opened the web browser. He typed in the little information he knew. Date, approximate time, costume, Victorian.

A fraction of a second later, his screen filled with results. At the top was an announcement of the Quarter's annual theme night.

He pushed the laptop away. Not much surprised him, but this left him shocked.

Mira Araceli, his partner, was on her way to the Quarter? *Fuck.*

How the hell had he not known they were members of the same club? Or that she was a submissive?

He shucked water from his still-damp hair. For a moment, he considered the idea she might be a Domme. It took him no time to dismiss that idea. When he kissed her, her response had been sweet. Instead of protesting his aggressiveness, she gave herself over to him.

There was no doubt she was a sub, and if she was going to the Quarter, she was looking for a Dom.

Torin shouldn't want to be that man.

The primal beast in him said *fuck that.* If she wanted to scene, she would do it with him.

Driven by urgency, he used an app on his phone to summon a ride. He didn't have the patience to take his own car, find parking, then walk a couple of blocks, even if the exercise might calm his temper.

Not giving a damn about the club's theme night, he locked up before jogging down the steps to wait for the driver.

A couple of blocks away from his destination, traffic snarled. Knowing he'd be faster on foot, he paid for the ride, then headed for the unobtrusive door on Toulouse Street.

The closer he got to finding her, the more impatient he became.

"You're supposed to be in costume, Master Torin," Trinity, the hostess, said by way of greeting.

"So it seems." The gentleman in front of him had been wearing an elegant frock coat and a top hat, and he'd been carrying a cane. Torin glanced down at his black jeans and scuffed boots. To complete his attire, he also had on a black bomber jacket. He couldn't be more inappropriate if he'd tried. "I didn't get the memo in time." After signing in, he pushed through the frosted glass door and strode into the main dungeon.

The place was packed, and he didn't immediately see Mira.

He checked the bar, where he'd spent the last three Monday nights, observing, but not participating. Tonight, though, would be different, from the moment he got his hands on her delectable body to the moment he took her home.

Caging his restless energy, he circled the entire dungeon, annoyed not to find her, but damn happy not to see her strapped to one of the Saint Andrew's crosses.

He pushed through the door that led to a quieter part of the club and gave cursory glances at the subs—male as well as female—who were attached to the spanking benches.

At the end of the row, he saw a woman kneeling astride one. She had the same long, strong muscles as Araceli, and her hair was a dark, tumultuous mess, with fiery highlights.

He kept moving, but faster.

It was her.

From the distance, he hadn't seen the color of the gown because of the stupid number of layers of muslin petticoats that were tossed over her waist. But now... Not only were her beautiful round butt cheeks exposed and highlighted by her choice of black stockings and a garter belt, but she was being flogged by Arthur Wilson. Thank God she was wearing a very modern thong. Otherwise Torin's temper might have unraveled entirely.

He had nothing personal against the man—besides the fact that he was wielding leather that was turning Mira's ass red.

Arthur caught her full-on with the flogger, and she

swayed her hips from side to side, not trying to escape, and instead, asking for more.

Right now Torin Carter was a dangerous man.

"Only a few more, pet," Arthur said. He drew back his arm again and soundly smacked Mira with the falls.

Mira rose up as much as the restraints allowed and arched her back.

"Next one. Ready?"

She nodded, wiggling, offering him more of her flesh, clearly loving every moment.

Even from a few feet away, Torin had heard the difference in the intensity of Arthur's next stroke. The man was taking Mira to more extreme pain levels. From her reaction, the blow had clearly stung as it was meant to.

Fury overcame reason.

Through the years, he'd played with dozens of women, many of them at this club. He'd enjoyed showing up and having a new woman kneel at his feet each time. But this was different.

A feeling of possession walloped him, squeezing his lungs as if a weight had been dropped on him. He'd never experienced anything like it before, and he fucking wasn't enjoying it now.

The woman on the bench was his partner. He'd kissed her. Last night, she'd braved the unknown to drag him from the throes of a night terror.

Despite the Quarter's rules, despite the fact that his partner was obviously a willing participant, Torin acted.

He grabbed hold of the smaller man. If Torin exerted a bit more downward pressure, the man would be on his knees. Part of Torin wished the other man would give him the excuse. "Playtime's over, Arthur."

Mira obviously recognized the sound of his voice. With a fierce scowl, she looked over her shoulder. A dental gag was shoved in her mouth, making it impossible for her to speak, but she was able to make frantic, desperate noises.

Torin glanced at the gathering crowd. There were plenty of Doms and subs captivated by the scene he was creating. Aviana's most trusted dungeon monitor stopped nearby and folded his arms across his chest.

Torin's focus was totally on the woman immobilized on the spanking bench. "Move along, boys and girls," he said to the Doms and the couple of Dommes who were still staring.

"Trouble?" Aviana, legendary owner of the Quarter, strode toward them with her usual willow grace. In keeping with the theme, she was dressed in Victorian wear, with her expected flair. Her gown was startling white with bright diamante accents. While she generally sported pink- or purple-colored hair, this evening the long tresses were silver. No doubt she wore her customary high heels, because she was looking him straight in the eye. Judging by her scowl, she was not pleased.

"Damn Carter interrupted my scene." Arthur all but sputtered the words as he struggled to pull away. "It's against club rules."

Aviana studied Torin. "By 'Carter,' I presume you mean Master Torin?" Aviana asked, maintaining decorum. Despite the tension, no matter what kind of situation, Aviana never raised her voice. Trouble in the club was handled professionally, defused by the power of the woman's mystery and magnetism.

Torin struggled to maintain his own composure. He was accustomed to being in charge, alpha even in a pack of alphas. But here, Aviana's word was law. Torin met the more controlled woman's eyes.

Arthur—Torin wasn't one to extend the courtesy of addressing the man as Master Arthur, no matter what Aviana insisted—had to tip back his head to look at them both.

"The woman Arthur's flogging—"

"Sub," Arthur interrupted. "At the Quarter, she's a submissive."

"The *woman*," Torin corrected, tightening his grip inexorably, "is my partner. As such, she is under my care and protection." More than anyone, Aviana would understand what that meant. She knew what he did for a living. More than once, he'd provided extra security for the club.

"Well, you're clearly not giving her what she wants, are you?"

Torin clamped his teeth together and exerted a bit more pressure on Arthur's wrist. "No one, *no one*, but me will be touching her."

Mira struggled against her bonds and made tiny mewing sounds.

With his free hand, Torin flipped the material of her dress back down to preserve her modesty.

"Perhaps we should ask the sub what she wants," Arthur suggested.

Aviana inclined her head. "Excellent idea."

Torin wanted to loosen Mira's bonds. Perhaps reading his intent, Aviana held her hand up, her palm toward him. "Stay where you are." She flicked a glance between the two men. "Both of you. Understand?"

He didn't nod until after Arthur did.

"Tore?" Aviana signaled to the massive, bearded dungeon monitor.

With a nod to acknowledge the order, the man closed the distance to Mira, then crouched next to her.

"Unfasten Ember," Aviana instructed.

Ember? It took him a moment to realize Mira must have used a scene name. But he liked it. A play on fire, for the highlights in her hair?

Tore unbuckled her first bond, and she flexed her wrist.

Torin struggled against the instinctive caveman act. He wanted to be the one to detach her, and ensure she was okay. Then he wanted to toss her over his shoulder, drag her up to one of the private rooms, and give her exactly what she wanted. Talking could come afterward.

Having no choice but to follow the club's protocol, he watched as the dungeon monitor unhooked the clips.

"Drop your flogger," Torin instructed Arthur.

"I—"

"If you don't," he said with a quick smile, "you'll be giving me a reason to break your fucking wrist."

"Master Torin!" Aviana rebuked. "That's quite enough. And Master Arthur, give that flogger to our DM."

Glaring, Arthur did as he was told, then Torin slowly released his grip.

Now that all of Mira's bonds were loosened, the dungeon monitor helped Mira from the bench and held on to her arm for a few seconds, obviously giving her time to catch her bearings and get her circulation back. Torin scowled. He'd meant it when he said he didn't want *anyone* touching her.

For a second she looked at Torin. Her brown eyes were wide, focused on him. She blinked, and then, seeming to recognize her error in staring at him, she dropped her gaze.

Jesus God.

How could he not have really seen her before now, not known what she wanted?

Tore secured her hands behind her back and then exerted pressure on her shoulders so that she knelt before them.

"Take out the gag," Aviana ordered.

The dungeon monitor unbuckled the dental dam and slowly drew it away and handed it back to Arthur. Mira swallowed several times, and Torin couldn't take his gaze off her.

On her knees, her head bowed, she was exquisite. And he was nearly undone.

"Quite the commotion you've caused, Ember."

"My apologies, Milady. That was never my intent."

Aviana's lips twitched. "Well, it seems you have two of our Doms very much interested in you."

"Yes, Ma'am."

"I take it, Ember, that you were willingly engaged in a scene with Master Arthur?"

Torin snapped his back teeth together. The Quarter might be Aviana's club, but Mira was Torin's partner. "Aviana—"

Mira interrupted Torin's protest, saying, "I was. Yes, Milady."

Fuck it to hell, Mira had just given Torin another reason to punish her.

"Go on."

"I approached Master Arthur when I arrived." She looked at Torin, then back at Mistress Aviana. Then, she went on, either not noticing or, more likely, ignoring Torin's clenched jaw, and he attempted to ignore the fact that Aviana cleared her throat to hide her smile. "He asked if I was alone."

"Goddamn it!"

"Last warning, Master Torin."

"Throw him out," Arthur encouraged.

"Stop goading him," Aviana snapped back. She returned her attention to Mira. "Master Torin states you're under his protection."

He figured he had another, oh, forty-five seconds of patience left. A minute, tops.

"Ember?" Aviana prompted.

"Well…"

"A yes or no will suffice."

Torin silently counted to ten, waiting for Mira's answer.

"I—" She looked at Torin. She swallowed. "We—"

"Choose wisely," Torin warned. He had no claim on her, and they both knew it.

But after that kiss, he had no doubt he wanted her as much as she wanted him. The question was, how much emotional risk she was willing to take. Scening together would bond them as nothing else could.

Despite his earlier demand that people move away, several couples had gathered closer to better hear what was being said.

Finally, after swallowing, she reached the right choice and said, "Yes, Milady. We're partners."

"Then the decision to engage in a scene with Master Arthur was not yours to make?"

Any other time he might have acknowledged Aviana's skill at defusing the volatile situation. As it was, with Arthur standing there, onlookers greedily drinking in the scene, and Mira on her knees, Torin wanted the drama to be finished and wanted her alone.

"Ember?" Aviana prompted.

"Technically he—"

"*Damn it!*" Torin snapped. "Answer the question."

She swallowed and then licked her lower lip. She tipped back her head and looked directly at Mistress Aviana, avoiding all contact with Torin. "No, Milady. As you said, the decision to give myself to Master Arthur was not mine to make." She bowed her head. "I'm sorry, Ma'am." She then looked at Arthur. "I apologize, Master Arthur."

Apologizing to the whiny bastard who'd been beating her? Torin closed the distance between them and dug his hand in her hair. Pins scattered across the ceramic-tiled floor.

Always the professional, no matter how much it pissed off Torin, Aviana crouched in front of Mira. Only the three of them could hear what was being said. Beneath his hand, Mira trembled.

"I'm going to give you a choice. I can turn you over to Master Torin, or I can call for a ride."

Torin tightened his fist in her hair and she rose up a little, as if to ease the pressure.

"Thank you, Milady." She drew in a shaky breath. "I was disobedient to Master Torin."

Master Torin. Goddamn, her words made his cock throb.

"I imagine he'll want to punish you."

She shivered. "Yes, Ma'am."

"You're fortunate I don't do so myself. I don't care for this kind of upset at the Quarter."

"I'll deal with her privately," Torin said.

"In that case, I believe it's settled?" With grace, Aviana stood.

"I'd like a private room. If you'll excuse us?"

"Of course. We'll ensure one is ready." She signaled to Tore. "Give us about ten minutes."

"Thank you." He nodded toward Aviana, then Arthur. Torin kept his fist in Mira's hair and exerted a small amount of pressure, ensuring her continued contrition. "I'd like a collar and a leash, also. Add it to my tab."

Mira gasped. He tightened his grip, silently warning her to keep quiet.

"It can most certainly be arranged."

Tore called over another DM while Aviana swept her arm wide and gave a smile befitting a monarch. "Please, everyone. Enjoy your evening!"

Loud, thumping music suddenly rocked the entire area. Tension eased and conversation around them resumed as people went about their business.

"No hard feelings," Torin said to Arthur.

"Fuck off." Arthur snarled. "How the hell was anyone supposed to know she was yours?"

How indeed?

Arthur rubbed his wrist. "Next time, claim your subs." He looked at the kneeling Mira. "And when you're done with this asshole, look me up."

Torin took a step forward.

Arthur glared at Torin before moving away.

"He's right," Aviana said. "Claim her. If this happens again, I will back whoever she is scening with. I did you a favor, out of respect for our relationship, but I consider us even. Don't cross me again."

With a tight nod, Torin acknowledged Aviana's order.

Within seconds the blond dungeon monitor returned with a collar and leash. "I'll take it from here," Torin said.

"Yes, sir," the man said, handing over the leather pieces.

Then it was just the two of them. She was still on her knees, and he liked that. "After tonight, we will still be partners, unless you request a transfer."

She nodded.

"Let's get a few things straight. I'm here now, and I sure as hell intend to beat you."

"Yes." The much, much softer, she added, "Sir."

His cock throbbed with need. Whatever it was between the two of them, it was real and potent. "Whatever you need, I'll make sure you get it." Torin captured her chin firmly between his thumb and forefinger. He forced her to look at him. "Beating, flogging, spanking, punishment, humiliation, bondage…" He trailed off. "I promise you. But there are rules."

"Such as?"

She was right, and smart, to ask.

"Until we mutually agree to end this relationship, you will not go to Arthur—or anyone else. Furthermore, you are not permitted to flash your bare ass at anyone without my permission."

"Let's just have this."

"Is that what you want?" He looked deep into her eyes. "Really? Or do you want to see where it goes?"

"A few hours. Then, afterward, we can reevaluate."

Unsatisfied, he scowled.

As if sensing his restlessness and unwillingness to compromise, she relented, just a little. "For the duration of our assignment, I won't visit the Quarter without telling you."

It was as much as he could hope for. "We will debrief after this." Words they both understood, a meaning that was clear to them. A discussion, pros, cons, what worked, what didn't, and what would be different in future.

"Of course, Commander." She nodded. "Give me what I crave, Commander Carter."

"Master Torin," he corrected.

"Give me what I crave, Master Torin."

CHAPTER FOUR

HAWKEYE

"Y ou're submitting to me?" he asked, pressing for answers so they were both clear. Consent was imperative. Without it, he wouldn't move forward. "Willingly?"

She took a breath and exhaled it in shaky measures. "Yes, Sir."

"Then, you'll wear this?" He held up the collar.

When she answered affirmatively, he secured the sturdy leather around her neck. He tightened it to the point he could get just one finger between her nape and the buckle.

She looked up momentarily. Her mouth was slightly parted, and her breaths were shortened, whether from fear or anticipation, he didn't know.

"I'm nervous," she confessed.

"I think that's what you want. Isn't it? The rush? Adrenaline? Uncertainty? Expectation? A touch of fear, maybe?"

"Is that meant to reassure me?"

"Not in the least."

"We've never played together before."

"If you think I'm playing now, think again." He placed his hands on her shoulders. "Now stand."

Since the gown was a monstrosity of length and fabric, and because her arms were still bound behind her, she struggled to comply. He made no move to help her. The usually graceful Ms. Araceli was out of her element, but to her credit, she didn't protest. When she stood in front of him, head bowed slightly, he said, "Good girl."

"I—"

"You look lovely." His cock had never been harder.

He fastened the leash to the collar's attached D-ring.

Torin liked having her at his mercy, on his leash, the black collar tight and stark against her delicate olive-toned skin.

From the beginning, Mira had fired a protective streak in him, one he'd never had for another woman. It was more than just their being partners—something much, much more.

He wrapped a hand around her upper arm to give her stability as they walked up the stairs to the private rooms. In those, there were fewer rules. The club's safe word would be honored, and DMs checked in on the scenes. Beyond that, nudity was okay, whereas it was forbidden in the rest of the dungeon.

He checked in with the DM who was in charge. "Room eight, Master Torin."

"Thank you."

When they were inside, with the door closed, he moved her to the middle of the room. "Limits?"

"What you might expect," she replied. "Bruises are okay." She smiled. "Hopefully they're more fun than the ones I received during training."

"I think you'll find them much more pleasing. Yes."

"No breaking the skin." She exhaled. "Nothing that will impair my ability to do my job."

He nodded. "Safe word?"

"Sangria."

"Sangria?"

"Sangria," she said. "It's red. At least traditionally, it is."

And it was a drink her country was famous for. Of course. And it fit with Ember. "What are your limits?"

"Permanent injury. Breath play. Knives. Unsafe sex."

"Nothing else?"

"No."

"You're an extreme player?" It wouldn't surprise him, with the way she approached life, as if everything was a challenge to be conquered.

"I have a safe word."

"Any problems with complete nudity?"

"Whose, Sir?" she fired back, lips quirking a little.

He grinned. The other night, she'd clearly not had any issue with him being naked. He wondered what her touch would have been like on his dick. Firm, no doubt. Araceli wasn't shy. "Yours, of course."

"I'm…" She hesitated, and he was glad.

Torin wanted her to think it through. He wouldn't be able to look without touching.

"Okay."

"Penetration?"

"With toys, fingers, yes. But… We may need to take sex as a separate subject," she said.

"Agreed." *Smart idea.* He removed the bindings from around her wrists then smoothed the red marks from her skin. Her pulse quickened. "You may want to thank me, lest I think you're ungrateful."

"Thank you," she repeated dutifully, respectfully. "Sir."

Before he got lost in her fathomless eyes, Torin unclipped the leash and curled it up on a nearby table. Then he went to work unfastening the dozens of tiny hooks and eyes that held her dress closed. He gave silent thanks that women didn't dress like this anymore. As it was, it took all his

75

restraint not to go barbarian on her and rip her out of the yards and yards of material.

When it was most of the way open, he drew the gown off her shoulders and let it fall to her waist. "Good girl," he said when he realized she wasn't wearing a bra. His cock was hard, demanding. He reached around to cup her breasts.

"Commander…"

"Sir. Or Master Torin while we're here," he reminded her.

"Master Torin."

"Much better. Are you protesting? Needing to use a safe word?"

"No." Her response was instant. "It's…"

"You trust me with your life. Here, you need to trust me with you emotions as well as your physical wellbeing. I promised to give you what you want. In return, you have to be honest in letting me know. There's no room for lies."

"You're turning me on."

"Good." Outside of the Quarter, he wasn't sure they would have ever gotten here. There was too much between them, real-world complications, of being partners, of her being his former student. He rolled her nipples between his thumbs and forefingers.

She moaned.

Even though they were well away from the rest of the club, nearby cries reached them, as did the bass thumping from the main dungeon.

He squeezed her nipples.

She moaned ever so softly.

He increased the pressure on her nipples until he knew it was painful.

Her knees buckled, but she caught herself and stood up tall before he said anything. "I assume that means you like pain."

She didn't answer.

"Araceli?" Then he frowned. "Or would you prefer I call you Ember?" It might be easier for her to separate her identifies that way.

"I go by Ember when I'm here."

"Like fire?"

Her eyes were already hazy. Slowly, she nodded.

It suited her. Very much.

He squeezed her nipples even harder, then instantly backed off.

She allowed her head to tip back, and her mouth parted.

"I asked you a question a moment ago. Do you like pain?"

"Yes." It was a whisper. A confession.

"I didn't hear you."

"Yes." Her word was louder, clearer. "Yes, Sir. I like pain."

He tightened his grip on her hard flesh

Though she moaned, she didn't protest.

"Tell me what you think, what you're feeling."

"Damn. I like it," she said. "It hurts. S-s-sir!"

"Shall I stop?"

"Oh heavens. No."

Eventually, he relented and released her. She sighed and her head drooped forward. Behind his zipper, his cock throbbed. Torin wanted to be naked, buried inside her.

He unfastened the final hook and eye that secured the dress at the small of her back. The fabric pooled on the floor. Next, he untied the ridiculous layers of petticoats and let them fall, as well. "Step out of the dress and everything else." Torin's voice was scratchy, more hoarse than he intended. *This woman...*

Her motions exaggerated and delicate, she did as he said.

She stood in front of him, almost bare. Even though she couldn't have known it, her choice in lingerie was perfect. Her black lace garter belt and silky, sexy stockings were the stuff of his fantasies. Her high-heeled, fuck-me shoes were definitely not around during the Victorian era, but they sure as hell turned him on now.

If he weren't careful, she'd bring him to his knees.

He shrugged out of his jacket and tossed it on top of the table. "Remove my belt, please." Since he didn't have his toy bag with him, his options for beating her were limited.

Her eyes opened a bit wider, but she reached for the buckle. "I can't help but notice your dick is hard, Sir."

And getting harder.

She took her time drawing the leather back through its loops. Torture. Pure torture. And undoubtedly deliberate.

With both hands, she offered the leather to him. He accepted, placing it on the table near his jacket. "Now that the dress isn't in your way, you may go to the far wall." After a short paused, he added, "On your hands and knees."

Her mouth dropped open. "You want me to crawl?"

"It's not a suggestion, Ember. It's an order. Do I need to repeat myself?"

She shook her head. "My stockings—"

"Can be replaced. Please do as I say."

She sank gracefully to the floor before moving onto hands and knees, doggy-style. She moved across the floor with a flawless class that made his dick physically ache. Her pert rear swayed slightly. He admired the length of her leg muscles, and he wondered how her thighs would feel wrapped around his waist.

When she arrived at the wall, she stopped and waited for further instruction.

"Stand and face it, please. Arms above your head. I want you totally flat against the bricks. Press your breasts into them. Be sure the concrete is scratching your nipples."

She hesitated only seconds before leaning in.

"I'm going to remove your panties."

Although she tightened her muscles, she didn't protest

as he worked the wisp of material down her thighs. In turn, he lifted each of her feet to remove the thong entirely. Since he didn't want to drop her underwear on the floor, he wadded the silk and stuck it into his front pocket. "Much better."

Mira closed her legs, as if that could protect her.

"Feet shoulder width apart." While she stood there, held only in place by the force of his will and her obedience, he grabbed two sets of restraints from the pegs on the adjoining wall.

He moved in behind her. "You're exquisite, Ember."

"Thank you…Master."

Master. He liked the sound of that much better than "Sir."

He crouched to wrap the restraints around her ankles and then secure them to the hooks in the floor.

He trailed his fingers up the inside of her right thigh. Her legs trembled. "Are you damp?" He drew a finger across her tender pussy lips.

She jerked and gasped, dropping her hands beside her.

"Keep your arms above your head," he instructed her. "You are damp. Will you still be like that after I use my belt on you? Or will you be wetter?" He slid his finger back and forth then pressed the pad of his thumb against her clit.

She jerked convulsively. "I… Please. I need…"

"On second thought, lower your arms. Reach behind you and spread your ass cheeks."

Slowly, she complied with his order.

For a moment, he closed his eyes to get control of his libido. Despite the fact they'd agreed not to have sex, he wanted to plunge deep inside her, slamming her against the wall, pounding out his orgasm, and taking her with him.

Intending to arouse her to the point she couldn't think, he teased her entrance.

Arching her back, she silently asked for more. For a long

time, he played with her before plunging a finger deep inside her.

With a whimper, she jerked.

Masculine pride rushed through him. He liked having this woman respond to him so completely.

Torin drew a deep breath. He was in control of the scene, and he intended to control himself as well. "How close are you to orgasm?" he asked against her ear. He moved his finger, and her internal walls constricted around him.

"It's been a long time," she said, her breaths becoming more and more shallow as he explored her insides. "M-Master Arthur warmed me up."

Torin growled and impaled her with a second finger. The idea of Arthur taking any liberties with this woman, *his* sub, infuriated him. "You're here with me now. You'll not orgasm without my say-so."

When she didn't respond, he asked, "Am I clear?"

"Yes, Master. But…"

"Problem?"

"I come easily."

"You'll come when I say you'll come. *Keep your ass cheeks parted!*" He knelt to lick her while he finger fucked her.

"Sir!"

He stopped short of letting her orgasm.

"Master Torin, you are impossible."

He grinned but was glad she couldn't see him. She delighted him, made him want to please her. "Did you have permission to speak?"

"No," she said.

"And…?"

"The sub apologizes."

"Apology accepted." He loved the way she referred to herself in the third person. She was into the scene as deeply as he was. "We'll just add another two lashes for insubor-dination."

She made a funny sound, somewhere between a mewl and a protest, but didn't say anything else.

He stood then pulled out his fingers from her, trying hard not to think about how badly he wanted to replace them with his cock.

He pressed a damp finger against her anus. Her muscles tightened, but instead of pressing forward and into the wall, trying to escape from him, she took a breath and pressed back in silent invitation.

Lust filled him.

He wanted her. "Bear down," he told her.

"Yes, Sir," she whispered.

As she followed his instructions, he pushed his finger in farther, past his first knuckle. She moaned and wiggled. Exactly the reaction he wanted.

"More," she begged softly.

He continued on, stretching her wider, sinking his finger all the way to the hilt.

"Mas...Master... May I come?"

"No chance." He pulled out.

She groaned in protest.

"Being impatient will prolong the amount of time until you are allowed an orgasm."

"I understand...Master."

After washing his hands in the nearby sink, he returned to her. "Arms spread, Ember. I want you properly secured."

Her shoulders rose and fell, as if she was breathing hard. Although she hadn't made anything ordinary off-limits, he knew he was pushing a boundary now. They'd never played together before, and all she had to operate on were her instincts. "I'm waiting," he said softly against her ear.

Deliberately, as if it were mind over matter, she moved her wrists higher.

Beating her was going to be a pleasure. The scent of her arousal made him that much more anxious to get on with it.

TORIN HAD BEEN RIGHT EARLIER. TO MIRA, SCENING WAS about the rush. The anticipation of knowing he intended to use his belt on her was like a drug, one she couldn't get enough of.

Realizing she was in danger of losing control, Mira called on her yoga practice and drew a breath deep into her lungs then exhaled it out in a controlled, measured way. When her nerves didn't calm, she did it again

"Right wrist first," Torin said, breaking into her thoughts.

His touch was uncompromising but surprisingly gentle as he secured her right wrist in place. Instinctively she pulled back on the tether, testing it. It was as unyielding as the Dom himself. A ripple of anticipation jolted through her body.

The wall was uncomfortably cold and the bricks scratched her tender skin. She was hyperaware of the room's chill, of the door with its window, of Torin's spicy, masculine scent.

He secured her left wrist in place, leaving her splayed and helpless.

Her pussy was still dripping, and her clit throbbed. For a moment, he traced the collar around her neck. Wildly, she wondered what it would like if it really was his, if he placed it on her as a sign of his ownership.

Scared by her own thoughts, she shoved the idea from her mind. It was ludicrous, something she didn't want.

"How many strokes with my belt?" he asked.

Uh. He wanted her to decide? A chill—part delight, part

dread—chased up her spine. Torin wouldn't let her abdicate her role in their play.

"Ember?"

"Eight, Sir?"

"Good place to start."

She shuddered.

"How many more for allowing Arthur to see you? And, worse, touch you?"

"When I invited him to play, I didn't realize I wasn't allowed to do that," she protested.

"That wasn't the question."

How could he arbitrarily enforce rules that she didn't know existed? It wasn't fair. Then again, nothing about their time together ever had been, starting with the training exercise at the nightclub. "Two."

"Three it is."

She opened her mouth but clamped it shut again. He'd simply add more strokes the more she argued. And since she didn't know how hard he would hit her, she figured she'd better err on the side of safety.

"How many total?"

"Eleven."

"You forgot the ones from earlier. The insubordination."

She sagged a little.

"So how many?"

"Thirteen." Quickly she added, "Sir" so he didn't add any extra for a lack of respect.

"Is your pussy still wet?"

"It was. Now I'm suddenly a little nervous," she admitted, "so I'm not as turned on as I was earlier."

He moved in behind her. Using his body, he pushed her hard against the cold, unyielding wall. She felt the scratch of denim and the hardness of his cock against her naked backside. Her breasts were flattened against the bricks. Her nipples hardened from her overwhelming arousal.

"I'm tempted to just fuck you with my hand while you're strung up here, totally helpless."

"*Now* I'm wet," she whispered. He didn't even need to touch her. He could turn her on just with words. He thrust repeatedly against her rear, simulating intercourse. She'd said no sex because it would be confusing outside of the club. But in this room, they could fuck, and maybe if they confined it just to here... More than anything she wanted his penetration, his possession. "Please," she begged. "Please fuck me."

"We need to discuss it when you're not so aroused."

His breath was warm, his body was hard, and his spicy, outdoorsy scent enveloped her.

"You'll count each stroke for me, *mo shearc.*"

His use of the Irish endearment undid her. It was easy to keep herself emotionally detached from him when she thought of him as her trainer and he called her by her last name? But referring to her with tenderness, in that tantalizing brush of a brogue...? She squeezed her eyes closed, as if that could keep him at bay.

He moved away.

"Damn it," she said. "Damn you."

The bastard actually laughed.

He left her weak and needy, on the razor's edge of fulfillment.

He caught her completely off guard, unprepared.

Torin landed the first blow, right under her buttocks, with a vicious upward stroke. She gasped from shock, from sudden pain.

His punishment had been much, much harder than she'd anticipated.

"Count," he reminded her.

84

"One," she bit out. There'd been nothing erotic about his first smack. Maybe he wasn't as fabulous as she'd thought.

He caught her again, in the exact same spot, with the exact same pressure.

"Ember?"

"Two." She braced herself as much as she could with nothing to hold on to.

The third followed suit, and it was then that she realized his skill. His aim was exact, his timing impeccable. He was a master of beatings.

"This is meant to satisfy all the nasty things inside you that you won't give a voice to. Unless I do this, you won't be happy."

He was so fucking right that she hated him.

"How many?" he snapped.

"Three!"

He added a little more force to the fourth, and she cried out.

"Four!"

"That's my girl."

For the next few seconds nothing happened. He allowed the time and silence to stretch. The only thing she was aware of was her own frantic pulse.

"Let me know when you're ready to proceed."

He thought she was struggling to take it? That annoyed the hell out of her. "Bring it on." She waited a couple of seconds before adding, "Commander."

"You haven't learned about goading me?"

Instead of hitting her, he tormented her, moving in closer, reaching between her legs, trailing his fingertips up her thigh…making her unravel.

He pinched her clit. She cried out. It hurt, but deliciously so. She ground her hips forward, all but trying to get off against the wall.

"Stop that. Naughty hussy."

She would have stamped her foot if it hadn't been shackled.

"Where were we?"

"Four," she said.

"Are you ready to resume?"

"Yes, Sir."

"More respectful. Better." This time he caught her across the fleshy part of her butt cheeks.

Damn it! "Five." It stung so bad. *Hurt so good.*

God, she'd wanted this. She'd wanted a man who could give her everything she needed. She liked the pain he inflicted, loved the fact he gave her a few seconds to savor the sensation before moving on.

"We have an audience," he told her. "Tore has been watching for the last few minutes."

That thought turned her on.

Before she was fully ready, Torin landed the next stripe across the uppermost part of her left thigh. The tip of the belt bit into her pussy. She moaned. She groaned. She wiggled, trying to escape. But he'd confined her perfectly, exquisitely.

He moved to her other side to catch her right thigh. Again, the end of the leather monster sliced against her exposed pussy.

"I can smell your heat," he said.

"Seven...and it freaking hurt, Sir."

"Bad?"

"Bad." Miserably, she nodded.

"Is that why your pussy is so wet?"

He added the eighth on top of the last two, as if tying them together.

"Tore is gone."

Torin's next three were perfectly timed and impeccably

landed. Each stripe was on top of the previous one, across her butt cheeks instead of the upper part of her thighs. They hurt like hell, and he wielded the leather aggressively. He gave no quarter, and she asked for none, wanting to feel the full power of his lash.

Each of the three blows dragged a scream from her.

She'd never been beaten so soundly, never felt so overcome with pain, with emotion. And yet, a small part of her realized they weren't done yet. She still had to take the ones for her earlier insubordination.

"You remembered."

And so had he, apparently. "I'm ready."

"I'm not." Instead, he scraped the prong of his buckle along the marks he'd made, digging into her skin.

It blazed torturously, pleasurably.

Her pussy was dripping from her arousal.

No other Dom had ever turned her on this way.

"I want your ass sticking out." Torin bent to unfasten her ankles then pressed his palm against her lower belly to move her back a little. "How are the bricks on your nipples?"

Because she'd moved each time he landed a blow, her skin had been abraded. "They're not as good as nipple clamps," she confessed, not believing she was admitting this. "But hot."

"Oh, Ember. The things I intend to do to you."

She wanted to experience all of them in their short time remaining.

"Thrust your hips out from the wall."

With her body secured, it was difficult to get into the position he'd requested, but she knew better than to complain.

Before her mind could assimilate, he spanked her, his open palm landing against her already raw skin.

Unbelievably his hand hurt far worse than the bite of leather.

"How many more, Ember?"

"Two."

"Ask me for them."

She wanted to sink into the oblivion of her thoughts, absorb the pain, make sense of it, savor it. But he wouldn't allow her that luxury. "Please, Master Torin. Please spank me."

"Where do you want them?"

"On my ass, Sir."

"Not on your cunt?"

Her insides constricted. For a moment she forgot to breathe. The idea of his powerful hand landing on her pussy scared her, thrilled her. And suddenly she had to know, had to know what it felt like, had to have the experience. "Yes," she whispered.

"I didn't hear you."

"Yes," she said louder. "Punish me there."

"Where?"

"My pussy," she said.

He played with her first, stroking her labia, teasing her clit, dipping a finger inside her arousal-slickened vagina. Her body convulsed. She was so close…

The first stinging blow made her gasp, made her even wetter.

"One more."

She moved slightly, arching her back, offering him better access to her private parts.

"Good girl."

His final slap forced her onto her toes. She cried his name.

Then she felt him behind her, his strong hands forcing her butt cheeks apart even farther, making her entire body strain.

He tongued her, and she screamed. She hadn't realized

he'd dropped to his knees. Relentlessly he continued, forcing her to fight an orgasm. She groaned and jerked when he pressed his thumb against her anal opening. The sensations were too much, pushing her beyond her endurance capability.

Mira needed the relief from the tension clawing inside her. "Master! Ohh, Master! I need to come."

He moved away from her and pinched the inside of her right thigh, but the distraction wasn't enough.

Then, without permission, breaking his rules, she shattered, pulling against her restraints, her hips jerking uncontrollably, her entire body shuddering against the rigid wall.

The orgasm was powerful, debilitating, every bit as emotional as it was physical. She was drained, her body limp in her bondage.

His presence overwhelmed her.

Though her eyes were squeezed shut, she pictured him, tight blue jeans—made even tighter by the size of his erection—scuffed and scarred boots, a black T-shirt with short sleeves, the fabric showing his powerful arms.

His scent was consuming, spice mixed with a hint of pure male sweat and the tanginess of a heated Southern evening.

But it was the way he'd beaten her that drained her completely.

He'd been relentless, demanding.

He made her hornier than she'd been in years.

"Ember?" he said, his tone was gruff, and it cut into her fantasies. Then, against her ear, he asked, "Did you come?"

She froze. She'd seen this kind of behavior before. Other Doms she'd been with had acted the same way, feigning shock and disbelief that she'd come without permission.

She knew intuitively that Torin would have continued to eat her, tongue her, press into her anus until she came. He knew how to touch her, how to encourage the response he desired. Torin Carter had forced her into a no-win situation. Still, Mira was startled into complete silence.

"Mo shearc?"

"Yes," she whispered. "Yes, Master Torin. I came."

"Most unfortunate. Now I'm afraid you really must be punished."

CHAPTER FIVE

HAWKEYE

Torin regretted staying away from her for so long.

Mira Araceli was utterly lovely, completely capti-
vating. He wanted to please her again and again. Her orgasm
had been as loud and unrestrained as the woman herself. Her
passion ran deep. She was everything he wanted. All the
things that scared the hell out of him.

Worse, he planned to fuck her senseless.

Which was complete madness.

Even if they didn't plan on it, sex would cloud their
working relationship. She fired a possessive streak in him.
One that should bother him.

After unfastening her wrists and rubbing the skin to help
restore circulation, he helped her back into her ridiculous
gown and the annoying petticoats or whatever the hell they
were called. He didn't, however, return her thong.

"Stand still," he said, working on the frustrating number
of hooks and eyes.

"Yes, Master."

The word rocked through him. Other submissives had
referred to him by the honorific, but until now, it hadn't sent

a burst of possessiveness through him. He fumbled the next hook. "Who was the goddamn idiot who thought up this outfit?"

She laughed.

"I'll ignore your rudeness. And in future, I'll keep you naked." His fingers were too big for the tiny metal clasps. In frustration, he skipped a few of them. Good enough.

They needed to debrief, but when he looked at her, her deep brown eyes were clouded. She wasn't quite back all the way.

Araceli might consider herself tough, but she'd also just had a scene. No doubt endorphins were still swimming through her system.

He grabbed his jacket from the bench, then draped the soft leather bomber over her shoulders. Only then did he feed his belt back through the loops on his jeans.

Torin picked up the leash and considered attaching it. Because of her earlier reaction, he figured they should talk about it before he compelled her to wear it. He made it into a tighter loop and stuffed it in his back pocket.

Then he scooped up his little submissive and her numerous layers of clothing.

Frantically, she kicked her legs. "Sir!"

"Settle down or I'll toss you over my shoulder."

"You would, too!"

"Of course."

He carried her from the room. As he started down the stairs, she turned into him and wrapped her arms around his neck. There were ways to get her to behave without an argument.

On the second floor, he shifted her in his arms, then sat on the velvet snuggle couch.

She tried to push away, but he held her tight. He wasn't sure why she had to be tougher than anyone, never giving in to human needs. As if she had something to prove. "It doesn't make you weak." She was the first recruit in the gym each morning. During training, she taped her ankle instead of having a medic check it out. She blazed forward, no matter the terrain or conditions. More recently, she'd been knocked upside of the head, and she'd refused Torin's assistance. Damn it, he wanted to protect her, make her feel cherished. He settled for, "You just had a hell of a scene."

"I'm okay."

"I'm sure you are." Then he took an emotional risk and admitted, "It takes me some time to come down too. Give me this."

She sighed. "Do you always have to win?"

"Does it really seem that way?" He turned her a little so he could study her face. "If so, I think you misread me. This isn't some move on an imaginary chessboard. It's real. It's about giving our minds and bodies to readjust to the real world." *After something so fucking sensational.*

With great reluctance, fighting his instincts, Torin relaxed his grip so she could escape if she needed to.

But that seemed to be exactly what she needed. Tension seeped from her. Her shoulders rounded, and she rested her head on him.

It was a powerful lesson. She needed to choose her own path, and her surrender was all the sweeter for it.

Hold on loosely.

He wasn't sure he was strong enough to do that.

Eventually, she splayed her fingers on his chest and closed her eyes. Mindlessly, he stroked her hair. Minutes later, their breathing synchronized. It was a powerful sensation, one he'd never shared with anyone else. "Mo shearc."

She might have dozed—but he doubted she would admit it—but some time later, she pushed herself away from him. Her absence weighed him down, a cold, physical thing.

"We need to debrief."

"Do we have to?" She sat up and scooted away from him.

"Afraid so. We can talk at the bar here. Or grab a coffee. Maybe a bite to eat if you need it. Or we can soak in the hot tub."

She leveled him with a hard look. "With swimsuits."

"Of course." Her fierceness made him smile.

"I think I'll be more comfortable talking away from here. I need to find Hallie to let her know I'm leaving."

"A friend of yours?"

"We came together."

"Do you need to do that alone?"

She hesitated for a moment. "No. But I might want a private moment, if she has any concerns."

He fished the leash from his pocket as he stood. Then he offered his hand to help her.

"Is that thing really necessary, Sir?"

"I say it is." Would she defy him? He watched a struggle play out on her face. It seemed she was a little bit of a masochist, but not into something she might consider humiliating.

Her safe word hovered between them. As he thumbed open the hook, he waited for her to resist or yield to his wishes.

Though she squeezed her eyes shut, she didn't protest as he clipped it to her collar. "It's stunning on you."

She met his gaze.

"You struggle with this. Why?"

"My training, I guess. If something goes wrong, I want to be free."

"You were fine during the scene."

"It doesn't have to make sense, does it?" She curled her right hand into the fabric of her skirt. "Being restrained while I'm bottoming helps me detach from the ordinary

94

world. I don't like to play in the main dungeon where there are a lot of people."

He nodded. "I've got your six."

"You're completely trustworthy."

Those words couldn't have come easily to her, which gave them even more weight.

"It's not about you or your competence, Sir. This is who I am. My experience of the world. I look out for myself."

"Have you always?" he asked, words soft.

"Commander—"

"Curious, that's all."

"My mother died when I was four."

From her file, he knew that. What he didn't know was how it affected her.

"She was lovely, an encouraging, gentle person. My father was…" She trailed off and clamped her lips together.

He waited.

"Former military. West Point." She shrugged. "Nurturing wasn't his way, or, rather, isn't his way. Tough love. All of us being compared to each other, as well as the children of his friends and colleagues. My brothers—both older—had it tougher than I did. My oldest brother followed our dad's footsteps."

"And the other?"

"Could never measure up. He tried, but it broke him. He has a…" She exhaled. "I have no idea why I'm telling you all this."

He appreciated that she was. "Go on," he invited.

"I guess you'd say he has a gentle soul. So much like our mom." She wiped a trembling hand across her forehead. "Or what I remember of her. He has a drug problem. Sometimes, he's on the streets. Dad has disowned him."

"Jesus."

Before he could say anything else, Mira held up a hand.

"Please. I don't want your pity. Save that for someone who deserves it. It wasn't a bad upbringing. We had a nice house, food, clothing, the best schools, all the advantages."

But not the one thing she craved the most? Her father's affection, and maybe more importantly, perhaps, his approval? Torin was fortunate. He'd grown up in a family of six kids, all of whom were loved deeply and encouraged to find their own way. It was loud and boisterous, and a firm foundation from which to explore the world. Love was abundant, even when he screwed up.

He lifted the leash several inches. "If this is too much to ask, I'll remove it."

"It seems important to you." Cleverly, Mira had turned his question around.

Because she'd revealed something about herself, he gave her an honest answer. "It pleases me to have others see that you…" He paused. *Belong to me.* "Are publicly acknowledging your submission."

"Master Arthur might still be here," she surmised. "And Mistress Aviana. Tore. Everyone who witnessed the scene. And this is how you can show you've claimed me." Not needing his confirmation, she nodded. "I understand."

She fucking tilted his world off its axis.

With her leash wrapped around his hand, they descended to the halfway landing. From here, there was an excellent view of most of the club, including *Rue Sensuelle*, or as it was colloquially known, Kinky Avenue.

As she searched for her friend, she scanned the occupied settings, a schoolroom, an office, a church. "She must be in the main club."

"Any sign of her?"

"Yes! She's watching that rope bondage."

With his hand in Mira's hair, they continued down the

stairs, then through the back area of the club to the door leading to the main dungeon.

Without stopping, he moved her toward the area she'd indicated. An expert was demonstrating a hogtie on a model, and Torin allowed Mira to lead him to her friend.

"You're Master Hottie," Hallie said.

"I'm sorry?"

Mira elbowed Hallie. "Uhm, that's my nickname for you." She shrugged. "I've seen you here before, and I didn't know your name."

He grinned, mostly at Mira's discomfort. "I'm flattered."

"Hallie, this is Torin Carter."

Her mouth fell open as she looked from Torin back to Mira. "That Torin Carter? Like your nemesis? The guy who was standing outside your door while you were busy stroking your—"

"I apologize, Sir. My friend seems to have forgotten all protocol."

"Partner!" Hallie corrected. "You're Mir—I mean Ember's partner. Right?"

"I prefer that to nemesis, yes."

"Will you excuse me for a moment, Sir?" Mira asked.

With a grin, he unclipped the leash and wound its length around his hand while Mira dragged her friend off to one side.

He wasn't close enough to overhear anything, but Hallie glanced his direction twice, her mouth open wider each time.

Less than a minute later, they returned.

"I'll call you tomorrow," Hallie told Mira.

"I'm ready, Sir."

"Nice to meet you, Hallie."

"I definitely need a job at Hawkeye," Hallie proclaimed before returning to the demonstration.

"After you," he said to Mira.

"Did you want to put the leash back on me?"

"I'm fine."

"Really?"

"Unless you want me to?"

She shook her head ferociously.

When they were in the reception area, he used his phone to arrange for a car. Then he removed her collar.

He offered it and the leash to her. "Will you put them in a coat pocket, please?"

"I should give it back to you."

"Keep it until we get home. I gave up on a few of those hooks on the back of your dress. You may need to preserve your modesty."

She grinned. "Before we leave, I need to claim my purse."

He joined her at the coatroom, resting his fingertips in the small of her back. As she waited for belongings, she stroked her forefinger across her throat where the leather had hugged her skin. Missing it? He could hope so.

AN HOUR LATER, HE WAS IN THE HOT TUB, JETTED BUBBLES dancing around him. Movement caught his gaze, and Torin glanced up at the carriage house to see Mira descending the staircase. She wore a white robe, and her hair was secured on top of her head with a clip that sparkled beneath a light.

As she walked across flagstones, moonlight bathed her with an otherworldly glow. Though he'd seen her naked, pleasured her, made her scream, she was as much of a mystery as she'd always been.

On the decking, she dropped her robe on a chair. Her bikini was skimpy enough that she might as well be naked. Her nipples pressed against the top, and the bottom didn't completely cover her buttocks.

With her toes, she tested the water. *A metaphor for your life, mo shearc?* Until now, he wasn't sure he'd met a woman whose secrets he intended to unlock. But he wanted to know everything about her. He wouldn't stop until he did.

"It's perfect." She held on to the rail as she entered the tub.

The evening was clear, with blessedly low humidity. It was a little crisp for New Orleans, making it perfect weather to soak in the heated water.

With a sigh, she sat, sinking to her neck. Then gently, she tipped her head forward and rolled her shoulders.

"How does your body feel?"

"None the worse for wear." She smiled. But she didn't use the word *Sir*.

They'd left their scene behind at the Quarter, and she hadn't asked for help when she removed the dress.

"You're an excellent Dom, Torin. Everything I could hope." She blew out a breath.

Studying her, he scowled. "You don't sound happy about that."

"I'm not."

He waited, giving her time to sift through her thoughts, perhaps choose her words.

"The truth is…" She scooted a little farther away. "I would have preferred it if you had been awful, limp-wristed, maybe. If you hadn't pushed me a little. With most play partners, eight strokes with a belt would have been ideal, but you insisted on more…" She took a breath. "Before you say anything, I know that I have a safe word. That's not my point. You pushed for more, adding the ones for insubordination. And something inside me soared. I like to be pushed, and you know me well enough to realize it."

"It wasn't a challenge." He'd been watching her, gauging where she was at. All of his actions had been calculated to give her what she wanted.

"I know." She swirled a finger on the water's surface. "The whole experience was better than I would have imagined. You were…" She exhaled. "I'm sorry. This is difficult to admit to myself, let alone out loud." More softly, she finished, "To you."

"Take your time. But I promise you this. You are safe with me." Still, she remained quiet. So he took the first step. "You were one of the most responsive subs I've ever been with."

"It was like—I don't know how this makes any sense, or maybe it sounds ridiculous—as if it wasn't our first time."

He wouldn't have put it that way. But she made perfect sense. Everything about the scene had been natural, seamless. "I get it."

"Maybe it's because we're partners. We've worked together and expect certain things from each other?"

Suddenly, he was unaccountably annoyed. "And maybe it's because it was just fucking right."

She wove her hand in and out of bubbling water. "Okay. What if we agree on that?"

"Then we have to figure out what the hell to do next." It wasn't against Hawkeye policy for them to be lovers. And plenty of people he knew had affairs with fellow operatives. A few even fell in love and got married.

"I want to have sex with you."

Hell's fury. His erection was instantaneous.

"But we need to agree on what it is. No attachments."

That feral part of him strained forward. "Meaning?"

"We're both physical people, Commander. And we are capable of separating emotion from copulating. We can do our jobs, go about our business. And if it's convenient, we can have sex."

"You're on dangerous ground, Araceli."

Steam rose from the water, and she waved a hand to disperse it so she could look at him. "Why?"

"I won't agree to your damn rules." He'd been rational at the club, but he was far beyond that now. "First of all, I don't fuck without it meaning something. You may have noticed I don't share well. And if you're my..." He looked at her pointedly. What was she? Words failed him. She was more than a hookup. Less than a girlfriend, but he wouldn't stake his claim any harder if she were. Torin settled on a word that was inadequate. "Lover, then you will not be sleeping with anyone else. If you submit to me, then I will be your Dom. Your *only* Dom."

"Our assignment ends soon."

As if he needed reminding. Soon enough, he'd back at the Aiken Training Facility with a new group of recruits while she was in the field. Long-term wasn't a possibility for either of them. Once again, he was unaccountably annoyed. His life was mapped out, and he enjoyed it. But now, the idea of being alone made the future look dark, unappealing. "I'm not flexible. I want to explore you, take you inside where I can make you scream and beg as loud as you need to. But I won't do it unless you agree to my terms."

Her response took forever, long enough for a vise to clamp around his heart and threaten to consume him.

When she spoke, her words were as cautious as he would expect from her. "If I agree to your terms?"

"Then I'll ask you how hard you want it." She didn't need to answer. This time, he knew what she would say.

"Take me inside?"

She was lucky that he didn't just bend her over one of the chairs and claim her outside. If the condoms weren't inside the carriage house, he might do just that.

He climbed the steps of the tub, then offered his hand to help her. She wrapped up in her robe, and he draped a towel around his shoulders.

When they reached their temporary home, he turned on a light, then locked the door behind them. "The robe, Araceli."

Her gaze fixed on him, she removed it.

"Now get rid of the swimsuit."

She sucked in a breath. "Yes, Sir."

That fast, they were back in their roles. Had she needed this from him all along?

Goose bumps dotted her skin as she reached to untie the strings behind her neck. Then she flicked open the front closure and let the top float to the floor.

Then, her gaze on him, she worked the bottom piece down. He wasn't sure if she was trying to tempt him or whether the material wasn't cooperating because it was wet. The end result was the same—it was taking her forever, and the torment made his cock so hard that his trunks could no longer contain it. "You belong to me."

Like him, she had a few scars, from the job and the rigors of training. They made her more exquisite. "Will you turn around? I want to see if your ass is still red."

Instantly, and with grace, she turned.

"All gone."

"Even the ones on my thighs?"

"Even those," he confirmed.

"I…"

"Need more?" He raised an eyebrow. "Lasting ones?"

"Yes." She took a step toward him. "I need you to fuck me."

Like oxygen, she sustained him.

"But first, do you mind if I shower? I want to wash off the chlorine."

He didn't mind at all. "I'll watch."

As if to instinctively protest, she opened her mouth. Then she closed it again, and her eyes widened with interest.

"After you," he said.

Mira bent to scoop her wet suit and robe from the floor, then led the way down the hallway to the bathroom. After depositing the garments in the laundry hamper, she turned on the faucets.

Since his last stay in the carriage house, the place had been remodeled. In addition to a clawfoot tub, an oversize walk-in shower had been installed. There was an overhead waterfall showerhead as well as a handheld wand.

Arms folded across his chest, he watched her stand beneath the spray.

Looking at him, she lathered the soap she must have used earlier, the one that reminded him of wildflowers. When her hands were completely covered in the bubbles, she returned the purple-colored bar to the little dish on the side.

Giving him the show he expected, she rubbed her palms over her breasts, making tiny circles, then taking turns lifting each to stroke up from the bottom.

It took all his self-control to be the stoic Dom when he really wanted his hands all over.

When she was completely covered in tiny bubbles, she reached for the handheld showerhead.

"I'll take that."

Eyes wide, she offered him the handle.

"Come closer to me." He started with her hands, then directed the spray over her chest and down her breasts before continuing lower toward her belly. "Spread your legs for me."

She sighed as he rinsed her pussy.

He could bathe her every day and not get tired of it. "I want to do your ass. Turn around and part your buttocks."

Mira swallowed deeply, but she whispered a respectful, intoxicating, "Yes, Master Torin."

Water sluiced between her ass cheeks, over her most private places. Soon, he realized his folly. Taking care of her was turning him on even more, and he was anxious to be inside her.

More quickly than before, he crisscrossed her body with the spray before replacing the showerhead and turning off the faucets. "Dry off and meet me in the living room. I'd like you naked and kneeling."

She nodded.

When she left, the wildflower scent still rich on the air, he stripped off and took a quick shower.

On his way back to the living room, wearing only a towel, he grabbed a condom.

She was waiting for him, kneeling on a small rug, head down, legs spread, and... *Fuck...* Wearing the collar. A sub had never pleased him more. "Come here."

Mira accepted his help up.

He plucked the clip from her hair, sending the long, luxurious strands tumbling around her shoulders. Then he grabbed a handful and pulled back her head.

Her eyes were hazed over. Anticipating his unspoken words, she parted her lips. Lost in her, Torin took her mouth. Her tongue met his, and he tasted the sweetness of her compliance. He was no longer capable of tenderness. Instead, he was determined to prove how much he meant his earlier words. Right now—if not forever—she belonged to him alone.

Torin thrust his tongue in and out of her mouth. With his kiss, he let her know what to expect when he fucked her.

As if she were made for him, she leaned into him, soothing all that was savage. She wrapped her arms around him and held on as if she'd never let go.

They were bare skin to bare skin. He dragged her close enough that her breasts were against him, her nipples hard, demanding nubs.

With reluctance, he ended the kiss. A hot desire for more

drove him. He dragged over a chair. "Put your palms on the seat."

Without hesitation, she did.

The air conditioner kicked on, swirling cool air over their still-damp bodies, making her nipples even harder.

When she was in position, she looked over her shoulder at him. Her eyes widened. "Damn."

He raised an eyebrow as he rolled the condom down his cock. "See something you like?"

"Ah. That's impressive. Even the other night... I... I had no idea you were *that* big."

"Problem, sub?"

She blinked alluringly. "I'll do my best. Sir."

"I've always admired your can-do attitude."

He strode toward her and placed his left palm on her shoulder. She sucked in a sharp breath. *Good.* He liked her being as affected as he was.

Torin skimmed his fingertips down her spine. Her head dropped forward, and her hair hid her features from him. She moved her body in response to his touch. He paused at the gentle curve of her spine. Then he used both of his hands to part her buttocks. "You like it hard."

"Yes," she whispered.

He slapped her right ass cheek. Instantly, he soothed the ache.

In silent invitation, Mira lifted up.

He played with her pussy, stroking her clit, sliding his finger gently in and out of her, making sure she was wet and ready.

When she whimpered, he moved in closer to place his cockhead at her entrance. She jiggled her buttocks. "Demanding, are you?"

"Dying." The word emerged on a strangled breath that he had to strain to hear. "There's a difference, Sir."

A little at a time, he inserted his length into her, sliding in, then back out.

"Please."

He filled her, and her internal muscles clenched around him. He tipped back his head and closed his eyes, fighting back his imminent orgasm. He should have beat off in the shower.

Focusing on her, he reached beneath her to torment her nipples, and she gasped. "Too hard?"

"No. Just, earlier, the bricks. I'm tender, and I'm on the edge of an orgasm."

"But you're not going to, are you? Not unless I give permission?"

"No. No, Sir." She panted when he tightened his grip and simultaneously pushed her breasts together. "Oh, Sir! I'm so, so close."

Torin continued his torment until she begged. Only then did he slowly release her, making her whimper in protest.

He changed positions, wrapping her up, one arm across her rib cage, the other across her upper chest. "I want you to stand up."

"Yes." She pushed off her hands, and he appreciated how physically capable she was.

As she eased upright, his cock sank deeper into her. When he was balls-deep, she gasped. "Too much?"

"No." She arched her spine, then slid a hand behind his neck for support. "I've been fantasizing about this for years."

"Years?" Her confession caused his cock to throb with incessant demand.

"Please, Sir. Please may I come?"

The knowledge that the attraction hadn't been one-sided made him drive up into her, hard, impaling her with his thrusts. It was raw, animalistic, filled with lust, and they were consummating a heat that had burned for years. For the moment she was his, and he'd leave her no doubt about it. "Yes. Come for me, my beautiful Mira."

Her body squeezing around him, she screamed.

Mira came in convulsing waves, and he tightened his hold on her as her hand slipped to fall by her side.

Her climax pushed him over the top. In a hot stream, he ejaculated, the orgasm ripped from the deepest part of him. It was both brutal and satisfying. But it wasn't even close to filling his desperate hunger for her.

She tipped her head back to rest on his chest, and he kissed the top of her head. He'd never had an experience like that.

Her breaths were labored, and she curled her fingers into her forearm. "Are you doing okay?"

For a moment, she didn't respond, and he was content to hold her, breathing in her scent. "That was everything I imagined."

He'd never been this complete.

And it wasn't enough.

He had to know every inch of her. "I'm going to take you to the bedroom." He stroked the column of her neck.

"Yes. Please, Sir."

CHAPTER SIX

HAWKEYE

Sometime in the middle of the night, Torin awakened to an empty bed. He wasn't surprised. The shock had been that Mira had fallen asleep in his arms.

After the edge had been filed off his urgency, he'd taken her to his room, secured her to the bedposts, fucked again, and then untied her so they could make love.

In her exhaustion, she curled up in the crook of his arm, for once letting down her formidable guard. He'd never wanted to let her go.

A gentle sound drifted on the night air, and he focused his senses, listening deeper, sifting out the background noises to discern what was different. *Water?*

He glanced at the clock. 2:47 a.m.

Perhaps she was exercising. But it wasn't loud enough for that. Curious, he pulled on a pair of sleep pants and went in search of her.

The lights in the main area were off, but the bathroom was bright. Water rushed from the faucet. Then suddenly, there was silence. The door was open a crack, and he knocked on it. "Mira?" Without waiting for an invitation, he entered.

She was chest deep in the enormous clawfoot tub, resting her nape against the rim.

"Room for me?"

"Are you serious?"

He dropped his pants, and she grinned. "I'll take that as a yes, then." She sat up to pull out the drain plug.

"Stay there." Behind her, he stepped into the tub. "Damn! It's hot."

As she had no doubt guessed, the moment he sat, water sloshed over the rim.

Together, they laughed, and it occurred to him that it might have been the first time they'd done that at the same time, from pure, stupid joy. Neither their jobs nor their personalities were given to light moments. Had he always been so serious? Or had events honed him?

When enough water had drained, she replaced the plug, then scooted back, trying to find a comfortable position between his legs. "You're ginormous, Commander Carter."

"We'll fit. It will just be tight."

"I think you like it that way."

"Your deductive reasoning skills are spectacular." He grinned.

"Hallie calls it spy shit."

"Could be more accurate than either of us want to admit." He laughed. "I like your friend."

"She doesn't have a lot of filters."

"It's refreshing."

"You weren't upset?"

"Not in the least. Come closer."

Surprising him, she did. He adjusted their positions so he could fold his arms around her. "Couldn't sleep?"

"I drifted off, for a short while." After a few seconds, she allowed herself to relax against him. "But then... Just a little restless, I suppose."

"Want to talk about it?" When she hadn't replied after a full minute, he tried again. "Did having sex bother you? Cross boundaries?"

"That's not it." She moved a hand through the water. "Or maybe it is. I don't regret it. It was freaking sexy. But..."

This time he waited.

"It was different than ever before. *Hell.* You seem to see me differently than anyone else ever has."

"You like to keep the real you hidden deep inside?"

"I'm not unique." Maybe because of what they'd shared, what she wanted him to understand, she didn't argue. "I think we all want to protect ourselves. At least to some degree."

For a while, the silence stretched between them, with only an occasional passing car disturbing the quiet.

"Even you won't let me see your vulnerabilities," she added. "It's safer that way." She placed her fingertips on an upraised knee. "Or we like to think so, right? Things happen, but we don't talk about them. Instead, we go through our lives hiding. It's less risky that way."

And maybe because of their intimacy, he didn't argue. "You're asking about my nightmare."

"You scared the hell out of me."

It had taken him hours to throw off the disorientation and shove the combination of memories and horrific imaginings back into the deep recesses of his mind.

"Does Hawkeye know how bad it can be?"

He'd been one of the only people Torin confided in. "He does."

"Have you talked to anyone? I mean a professional."

"I did. Hawkeye didn't give me a lot of choice." The dreams had been fewer and further between, less intense. Until Mira. "My partner was killed in the line of duty."

"I…" Her body went rigid, and he stroked her shoulder reassuringly. "Sorry. I had no idea."

Mira pulled away and moved to the far end of the tub. When she was as far away as possible, she turned around to face him.

Sex with her had been damn good for him too. Until he was inside her, he'd had no idea how much he craved human contact. Not just anyone. *Mira.* She hadn't needed to save him from the nightmare, then stay with him until he was out of its throes, but she had. Seeing her with Arthur had flooded him with rage, an emotion no other woman had triggered in him.

She was owed an explanation. No longer hiding, he met her beseeching gaze. "Her name was Ekaterina. We were working security at a football match—soccer to the rest of the world. In Mexico." Time hadn't diminished the memories, the colors, screams, chaos. In fact, it had sharpened each image, fine-tuning them with details he'd missed on that bright, cloudless day. "There was a duffel bag on the ground next to a trash can. Black. Canvas." He could recount the brand name, the exact dimensions.

Torin called the authorities.

He and Ekaterina were instructed to clear the area without causing undue panic. "There was a man who pushed past her. Ekaterina must have assumed he was a good guy. Instead of calling out a warning, she threw herself on the bomb. He detonated it remotely and took them both out."

Mira wrapped her arms around her knees. "Oh, Torin."

"If we had kept the perimeter like we should have…"

"That's a horrible thing to live with."

"There should have been something I could do to stop her."

"It might never make sense."

That was the worst thing of all. No matter how much time passed, regret and recrimination would follow him. "Come back to bed with me?"

A tiny furrow appeared between her eyebrows. How much was she willing to risk? She hesitated long enough that he straightened his back, steeling himself for her rejection.

"I'd like that." She offered a slight, half-smile. "Make it worth my while?"

"What have you got in mind?"

"I'm sure we'll think of something. Sir."

———

"Breakfast?" Torin offered, opening the passenger door of his car.

Mira blinked, trying to moisturize her gritty eyes. It'd been a hellaciously long night. A popular starlet was getting married the following weekend, and as a last hurrah, she and seven of her bridesmaids had decided on New Orleans as stop one of their blowout bachelorette party.

They'd hopped in and out of bars, no matter how dubious they were. At three a.m., the bridal party—laden with Mardi Gras beads from flashing their breasts—had staggered into the Oubliette, a dive located off a fog-filled alley. After a round of cocktails labeled A Short Trip to Hell, they had wanted to grab food—compliments, no doubt, of the entire can of energy booster in each drink.

It had been almost six a.m. when she and Torin saw them safely onto the elevator.

"I'm not sure what I want more," she admitted when

Torin slid behind the wheel. "A shower. Sleep. Or food. That was one of the most challenging assignments ever."

"We needed more people. Who knew that eight women could be so much work?"

With a grin, she tipped her head back. Especially when one of them was so beloved and instantly recognizable.

"Some of them are going to regret the pictures on social media."

No longer their problem. And the Hawkeye team in Las Vegas would have their hands full tonight when the bridal party landed at McCarran International. "Breakfast," she decided.

He turned toward her. His blue eyes were narrowed and laced with promise, and maybe a layer of threat. Despite her exhaustion, nerve endings lit up.

"I can make sure you sleep well."

She slid a little lower in her seat. No doubt he was right. And all of a sudden, she was thinking about skipping the chicken and waffles.

"Sustenance," he decided for both of them, checking the mirrors before driving out of his parking spot. "I want you conscious when we have sex."

His words and their inflection aroused her.

"Then we can pass out for a week."

"Wouldn't that be nice?" And unlikely. Over the past week and a half, she'd realized that he slept well, but only if she was in his bed.

Torin's emotions were stoked like a furnace. He was possessive and demanding.

Consuming.

Yet she wasn't strong enough to stay away from him, even though she knew he would eventually break her heart.

After clearing an intersection, he placed his hand on her

knee. The gentle nonsexual touch ignited a flame that would burn until they arrived home.

Over breakfast at the Shamrock Grill, something that was becoming a tradition, they debriefed. After filing an update with Hawkeye from her cell phone, they marked themselves as unavailable for another mission for twelve hours.

When the bill came, he reached for it.

"I think it's my turn." Besides, she'd had extra chicken and juice as well as coffee.

"Oh. I insist. I wanted you to have energy, so this is all about me."

She grinned. "In that case, take me home, Commander."

The French Quarter was just waking up as they walked back to the car. The driver of a beer truck was loading cases of local brew onto a dolly. They cycle never ended, and already, some intrepid tourists were already out, making their way to Café du Monde for a plate of three perfect beignets.

Five minutes later, she and Torin were headed back to the Garden District.

He stopped in front of the estate to open the garage. "It's been too long since I've had you across my lap."

Of all the positions they used, that was her favorite.

"And enjoyed your screams."

Her mouth dried. It was as if her cries sustained him.

"Mira?"

His voice, with its hint of a rich brogue, dragged her from her reverie. While she was lost, he'd parked the car. She gave him a slight smile. "Yes, Sir."

He followed her up the stairs, then locked the door behind them when they were safely inside.

Torin swept his heated gaze over her, and her heart thundered.

He took off his jacket and tossed it over the back of the

couch. Then he crooked his finger and pointed to a spot on the floor in front on him.

Her mouth dry, she stood where he indicated and remained still while he helped her out of her blazer. Taking care, he placed it on top of his.

She'd worn a slim-fitting tank top. Keeping his gaze on her, he fisted the material, then dragged it over her head.

"No bra?" Roughness gave his words a biting edge.

"It's built in."

He groaned. "Don't ever do that to me again, Araceli."

"No, Sir." *Until our next assignment.*

She toed off her boots while he unfastened her pants and lowered the zipper.

"Jesus. God. Mary and Joseph."

Normally she reserved her sexiest panties for time off, but his reaction was worth it. She lowered her head to hide her smile.

"If I'd had any idea what was beneath your clothes… All that lace?" He grabbed her pussy through her panties. "So wet for me." He squeezed hard, painfully, arousing her to the point of screaming her pleasure. "Fuck, yes."

He stripped off her panties, and she quickly undressed him. "My bedroom, Araceli."

As he customarily did, he followed her down the hallway. For fun, she gave an exaggerated butt wiggle before flashing a wicked grin over her shoulder.

"Oh, Araceli. I can't wait to have my hands on you."

She walked a little faster.

In the room, he sat on the edge of the mattress. "This is for fun. And for no other reason."

"Yes, Sir." She draped herself over his lap, then braced her hands on the floor. Without instruction, she parted her legs slightly.

He light strokes, he played with her clit, making her squirm.

Without giving her any warning, he slapped her pussy hard.

She gasped. "Yes." Her whole body lit on fire. With a sigh, she moved back into position.

Then he spanked her in earnest, on her buttocks, on her pussy, on her thighs. They were timed to arouse her, driving her to the brink.

Within a minute, she was begging for an orgasm. "I need..."

"You need?"

"Fuck me, Sir." Her words were breathless. "Fuck me. Please?"

"How do you want it?"

"Anal."

Torin helped her off his lap and stood her in front of him. "You're serious?"

He'd fingered her there, and a couple of times they'd used butt plugs, but she'd never asked for it. Tonight, she wanted it rough.

His eyes were narrowed, and his cock jutted forward, hard and with a drop of pre-ejaculate glistening on the tip.

"Give me a second." He grabbed a condom and a bottle of lube from a dresser drawer.

She forgot to breathe as she watched him roll the condom down the length of his impressive erection. Involuntarily, she shivered. Having that inside her tightest hole was going to be a challenge.

"On the bed," he instructed. "Facedown." He grabbed a pillow and helped her to place it beneath her belly. "Do you have any idea how red your ass is?"

"If it looks like it feels, yes, I have an idea."

"It's lovely." He spanked her again on top of a couple of

the welts, and she moved against the mattress, trying to achieve satisfaction. "Mine," he reminded her. Then, the perfect Dom, he placed a hand between her legs.

"Oh, Sir!" Desperately, she thrust her hips back. "Take me."

"Every part of you, mo shearc."

She turned her head to watch him squirt a dollop of lube onto his fingers.

"You're going to like this. Even if it's uncomfortable."

Especially then.

Slowly he inserted one slick finger into her anus, allowing her time to accommodate his touch. "Relax," he said, sweeping her hair from her neck, tangling his fingers in it.

Mira closed her eyes and concentrated on her breathing.

"Ready for more?"

"Yes." She nodded.

He inserted a second finger, followed by a third. He stretched her, holding his fingers apart. It hurt, not badly, but enough that she wanted him to back off. She was going to ask him to stop, but he leaned over and kissed her exposed nape, distracting her.

"You're doing well, Mira."

A hundred pleasurable sensations danced down her spine.

He was attuned to her reactions. The second she relaxed and surrendered, he began to move in and out, simulating sex as he lubed her channel and widened her even more.

"Yes," she finally said. "I want your cock."

With deliberation, he withdrew his fingers. He caressed her for a short while, then promised to return in a few seconds.

While he went to the bathroom to wash his fingers, her body cooled, and tension started to creep through her. She was edgy, with adrenaline flooding her veins. She'd never been more alive.

"On all fours," Torin instructed when he returned. The mattress sank as he knelt behind her. "Head down, and arch your back."

When she was situated, he held her ass cheeks apart and pressed the yielding firmness of his cockhead against her opening. "Bear down." He eased forward.

"God!"

Slowly, he withdrew, just a little.

It didn't give her any relief.

"Doing okay?"

"Yes," she lied. He was so hard, and this was far more intense than she'd imagined. "Just take me."

Torin proceeded at his own pace, claiming her in slow measures, starting with shallow strokes, then going deeper a little at a time.

"Will you spank my ass, please?" Anything to distract her.

He did, and the sharpness of the pain took her focus way from the way her anus burned, heightening her pleasure immeasurably.

"Stroke your clit, Araceli."

With his possession and her angle, that wasn't easy.

"Sir—"

"Do *not* tell me no," he warned.

She loved it when he was relentless with her. The fact that he'd demanded it meant it was possible.

Somehow managing to keep her balance, she toyed with her clit. He continued to spank her and occasionally reach beneath her to toy with one of her nipples.

Her vision swam, colors swirling, red and purple.

Torin drove his entire length inside her, forcing her forward. If he hadn't grabbed hold of her waist, she would have pitched forward onto her stomach.

He paused while she got back into position. "That's it."

Now that she had accommodated him, her nerve endings hummed with pleasure. "Do me," she pleaded.

"Goddamn, Araceli." He rode her hard, pulling all the way out and then surging forward, again and again, fiercely claiming her.

Faster and faster, she stroked her clit. Her legs trembled as she thrust back into him. Then her world fractured. Powerful and unexpected, an orgasm crashed into her. She screamed his name.

"Hell," he whispered, stroking her. "You're sensational."

"I want you to come."

He placed one arm beneath her hips, holding her immobile as he continued to ride her.

Even though she was sore, his pleasure nourished her.

He shortened his strokes, and his breathing changed. His grip on her tightened, as if he were a desperate man.

Inside her, his cock swelled. "Sir... Master."

His body went rigid, and he came in long pulses, and he growled with pure male satisfaction.

She wasn't sure how much time passed—seconds? A minute?—while he stroked his fingers down her spine.

When he withdrew, it was as if their emotional connection was also severed. She scoffed at her own ridiculous idea. Torin wasn't the kind of person to run or to abandon her.

"Stay right there."

"I should shower."

"You should wait," he countered. "I'll be right back."

Of course the badass alpha would insist on caring for her. She made a small attempt to smile, but she couldn't even manage that much.

He left, and she buried her face against her forearm. Even though she'd just given herself a pep talk, his absence left her bereft.

What the hell was wrong with her? She took a breath,

telling herself it was hormones after something so intense. Malfunctioning brain chemistry.

It had to be because there was nothing else between them. They worked together, scened together, and that was the nature of their agreement.

No matter what, she couldn't allow herself to get lost in Torin Carter.

CHAPTER SEVEN

HAWKEYE

"Black tie required," Mira said when she hung up the phone.

From his place on the couch in the carriage house, Torin raised an eyebrow. "As in a tuxedo?"

"Yes. Seriously. That was Ms. Inamorata herself."

He whistled. "I don't suppose you know her first name?"

She laughed. No one knew Inamorata's first name. Hawkeye's right-hand woman was damn good at everything she did, and that included keeping secrets. The office pool to guess her name had five figures in it. Whoever won would have enough money for a heck of a vacation or a down payment on a house. "If I knew, I'm not sure I'd tell you."

"So you wouldn't want to take me to Greece with you?"

"Greece?" All of a sudden, she was on a lounge chair on a white sandy beach, drinking a frappé while Torin stretched out next to her.

She shook her head to banish the image. They didn't have a future. Letting herself think about one, even momentarily, would lead to heartbreak.

"Araceli?"

Torin's voice penetrated her haze. "Sorry?"

"Where are we headed?"

"The Maison Sterling. Trace and Aimee Romero have a personal security client attending a fundraiser." In addition to being recently married, they were both well-respected agents. Aimee was the younger sister of the enigmatic Ms. Inamorata. A brainiac if there ever was one, Aimee was a scientist who had recently taken up running ultramarathons. The extreme running thing made Aimee's brainpower somewhat suspect, in Mira's opinion. "In the last few minutes, there's been a credible threat against their client."

"Anyone I know?"

"Nathaniel Sinclair."

He whistled and nodded. "No wonder they're calling in backup."

The man was a media magnate. He owned newspapers, magazines, a cable network, and there was a stadium named after his family. He wasn't popular with everyone, though, and there was no shortage of people who would like to prevent him from becoming President of the United States. "Inamorata is emailing the hotel layout to us." Even though Mira had been to the hotel for happy hour, she wasn't familiar with the ballrooms. "Evidently, he refuses to be seen as weak, so he's sticking to his original plans. He'll be arriving at the front entrance, and press is expected."

"Hence the dress code."

They needed to blend in, not look like security.

"When are we due there?"

"The party starts at seven. Inamorata wants us there by five." She checked her watch. "That gives us about an hour to get ready. I think I'll take a shower."

"I'll join you."

She looked at him pointedly. "And then we'll be late."

He swept a gaze over her, as if calculating whether they should take the risk. "You're probably right."

Mira was glad he agreed, because all of a sudden, she was tempted.

"A hot tub and a scene after we get back?"

"I'll look forward to it all night."

He headed for his room but stopped in the doorway. Mira ordered herself to continue past him, but she didn't, because the only thing she wanted was to be in his arms. "Shower," she said aloud, reminding herself as much as him.

"Shower," he affirmed, taking hold of her shoulders.

He claimed her mouth, kissing her deeply. He tasted of coffee tempered by a hint of cream, then drizzled with sin.

She couldn't resist him.

Responding, Mira lifted up onto her tiptoes and wantonly grabbed hold of a fistful of his black T-shirt. He pressed his free hand against the small of her back, holding her tight. She wiggled about a bit, growing more and more aroused beneath his sensual assault. Torin Carter made her want to be *very* naughty.

Very slowly, he ended the kiss. Her mouth was raw and ravaged, ensuring she'd spend their night hungry for more.

Torin looked at her intently. The color of his eyes never failed to startle her, but now she read the heat of arousal in the smoky blue depths.

"Shower," he said, letting her go.

Despite the time pressing in on them, it took her a couple of minutes to shake off the effects of his dizzying kiss.

He knocked on the door. "I'm going to think you're taking so long because you want company!"

Mira quickly finished up. After she wrapped a towel around her, she opened the door.

He stood there, naked, erect.

Her mouth dried.

"Figured I'd undress to save time. Bad strategy?" His slight grin made her tummy flip over.

"You're impossible, Commander Carter." She ducked to dodge past him. When she reached her room, she closed the door.

"Araceli?" he shouted. "Skip the underwear."

She laughed. There were ways their D/s relationship crossed over to their professional life. But the truth was, it was so unobtrusive and such a turn-on that she didn't mind. In fact, she would miss it when she had a new partner.

When she didn't respond, he called out, "Excuse me?"

"I heard you!"

The shower water turned on. "And what you meant by that was, 'yes, Sir.'"

Her grin only deepened. His challenges were sexy, and she looked forward to them. "Yes, Sir!" she called out dutifully. And she skipped the underwear. She wouldn't tell him, but the dress looked better without them, anyway.

After she was ready, she transferred her identification and a credit card to her dressy handbag. She double-checked that her gun was loaded, then placed it inside a special interior compartment. Finally, she added her stun gun and her cell phone.

By the time she was in the living room, Inamorata had sent over a 3D rendering of the ballrooms and service areas, including kitchens.

Mira printed them out and placed them on the kitchen table to study them.

Moments later, he joined her, and he was adjusting one of the cuffs on his snow-white shirt.

Damn. Her heart dropped to her toes. His hair, the color of midnight, flirted with his collar. His eyes seemed all the more electric against his dark clothing. In a tuxedo, with a fresh shave, he was devastating.

He perused her, as if drinking in every nuance. "Show me," he said.

"Show you?"

"That you followed my command. Bend over."

"Torin…"

"Bend over, Araceli," he repeated in a tone that allowed for no argument. "And lift your dress."

Unable to deny him anything, she turned around and exposed herself to him

"Lovely."

Against her will, her pussy became slick. He walked to her, footfall firm, a staccato threat.

He stroked her, finger-fucked her, then gently spanked her vulva until she whimpered.

"That will have to hold both of us over for the foreseeable future."

He smoothed her dress back into place. After she stood, she brushed imaginary wrinkles from the fabric.

"Are those the blueprints?"

She shook her head to clear it. "Yes."

Like she had, he picked up the pages, studied from different angles, committed the schematic to memory.

He snagged the vehicle keys off a hook. "Shall we?"

"Are we driving?"

"I figured we can valet park at the hotel. We're early enough that none of the principals will be there."

"And we can expense the cost."

"There is that."

As they approached the French Quarter, Inamorata sent a text message. "We're meeting in a suite. Third floor."

When they were inside the hotel, Torin cupped her elbow and led her toward the elevators.

Inamorata responded instantly to Torin's knock and invited them in. As usual, she wore a pencil skirt, and her hair was pulled back. Surveillance equipment covered the large table. She handed each of them an earphone, and a technician secured the radios in place.

Afterward, Mira and Torin each went through a sound check.

When everything was satisfactory, Inamorata continued on, outlining the plan in her usual straightforward way. "You're a couple tonight. Aimee Romero will be arriving with Mr. Sinclair. She'll be posing as his date for the evening. Trace will be arriving in a limo at approximately the same time as Sinclair so that he's onsite without arousing suspicions."

"Got it," Mira acknowledged.

"Cocktails are in fifteen minutes. When you arrive, hotel staff and a few members of Mr. Sinclair's staff will already be onsite, including his campaign manager."

"Who's verifying the guest list?" Torin asked.

"Sinclair's executive assistant. She should know people. Laurents will be nearby in case she notices anything amiss. Barstow will be stationed at the back of the room, near the entrance. He'll be close enough to assist either you or Laurents should the need arise. Here's your official invitation."

She handed over the sturdy hand-addressed card to Mira, who tucked it into her handbag.

"Let's use the service elevator. I want to show you the kitchen and the ballrooms."

Even when blueprints were available, Hawkeye Security preferred their agents walk a venue when possible. Seeing a picture was different than being in a room that was prepped for an event. Knowing where the exits were and how to use the back of the house to move the principal if necessary could save time and lives.

"After that, I'll introduce you to Sinclair's staff. We've

timed it so that you'll be among the first at the event so you can watch all of the arrivals. Any questions?" At their silence, she gave a sharp nod. "In that case, come with me."

AT ONE MINUTE AFTER SEVEN, TORIN PLACED HIS FINGERS intimately in the small of Mira's back and guided her toward a space cordoned off with velvet ropes. "Showtime, Ms. Araceli."

Sinclair's assistant pretended to look at their invitation before putting a checkmark next to their names on the official guest list. "Enjoy your evening," she said with a genuine smile.

Before they proceeded into the reception area, Torin nodded toward Laurents, their fellow Hawkeye operative.

Since party nominations were still more than a year away, Sinclair hadn't been afforded Secret Service protection. But Barstow—stationed at the back of the room— looked rather official.

Even though only one other couple was already in attendance, a live band played forties music, and champagne flowed freely. Obviously no amount of money had been spared.

Though Torin and Araceli each accepted a flute from a server, neither took a sip. Instead, they found a tall table near the entrance and watched as guests arrived. At first, it was a small trickle, but around seven thirty, crowds flooded in. Still, nothing looked unusual.

Just before eight, agent Trace Romero walked in.

Moments later, there was a buzz of activity near the door. Music ceased. Paul Kauffman, Sinclair's campaign manager, took to the stage and accepted a microphone. "Ladies and gentlemen, please welcome the next President of the United States, Nathaniel Sinclair!"

Shouts of approval and loud claps filled the room. The mogul came in with a wave, Aimee at his side.

Sinclair made his way to the stage and said a few words of thanks. He seemed completely at ease, without a care in the world.

Immediately creating a security nightmare, he left the stage and started glad-handing all the attendees. People queued up to meet him, blocking a smooth exit. Torin figured Aimee would unobtrusively move Sinclair toward safety and keep her body between him and the guests as much as possible.

"I'll be back," Mira told him.

"Araceli—"

"That man…" She leaned in closer to him so she could be heard above the din. "About six foot two. Blond. He came in after Sinclair when there were a bunch of people. I'm not sure he was cleared. He could be fine. I don't know. Check him out." Without waiting for him to respond, she walked away.

Frowning, he went to talk to Sinclair's assistant.

At the doorway, Torin looked back to see Araceli change directions, veering away from the man and toward a woman who was in line to talk to Sinclair.

He paused.

Araceli took hold of the woman's hands, as if they were old friends.

A slow alarm beating in him, he waved to Laurents. "We need to go over the guest list," he said to Sinclair's executive assistant.

Then, even though they were some distance apart, Araceli's voice rose above everyone else's.

Awareness prickled at his nape. Something was off. He keyed his mic. "Everything okay, Araceli?"

She didn't respond.

"Laurents, take over here. I want to know who Araceli's talking to. And she was interested in that blond guy." He pointed. With a nod, he started back toward Mira. He keyed his mic. "Heads-up, team. Blond male, six-two. Twenty feet from our principal. Araceli's on a brunette."

"Roger," Barstow acknowledged, making his way toward the target.

Trace also confirmed the transmission.

Looking like an attentive girlfriend, Aimee slid in closer to Sinclair.

Torin neared Araceli. Her voice was even louder now, with a fake, gushing tone woven through it. "I'm sure I've seen your picture before. You look so familiar. Are you famous? You are, right?" Mira inserted herself in front of the brunette.

Her stiff smile, obviously surgically enhanced, started to fade. "You're mistaken," she snapped. "Get your hand off me!"

"May I have your autograph?" Mira asked. "You will make me so happy. Please?"

Torin moved in next to Mira. "Everything okay, honey?"

"She's a movie star!"

"I'm sorry." Torin shrugged, as if he were a helpless male while he tried to see the world through Mira's eyes. "She's an autograph hound. If you'll humor her…"

A sheen of sweat dotted the brunette's upper lip.

"Wait! I have a pen right here," Mira said. She opened her purse. "Oh. No!" She got louder and more animated. "I don't have one. What am I going to do? Do you have one?" she asked the woman. "Can I borrow yours?"

She was drawing the attention of a lot of people, and Aimee whispered something in Sinclair's ear, then kissed him on the cheek, looking like a lover who was anxious to have her man all to herself.

"Darling, I'm so excited! She's going to sign an autograph!" Mira babbled to Torin.

The brunette snapped. "I don't have a pen."

"Just look," Mira implored. "Please?"

Her expression more a snarl than even a politely civil smile, the woman made a show of opening her pocketbook.

Mira acted. She jostled into the woman, forcing her to loosen her grip on the purse.

Metal glinted in the overhead lights

Fuck! Torin keyed his mic. "Gun!"

Pandemonium erupted, and hysterical screams rent the air.

Aimee and Trace hustled Sinclair toward a side door.

The brunette grabbed the revolver. Before he could act, Mira surged forward.

The gun discharged. The percussion deafened him, and he was helpless as the bullet ripped into Mira.

CHAPTER EIGHT

HAWKEYE

Pain shredded through Mira, glazing her vision and throwing waves of nausea through her. But they did nothing to stop her determination.

With focus borne from months of relentless training, she shoved aside survival instinct and put all of her kinetic energy into taking the brunette down. Blood dripped everywhere, and her upper arm burned, but Mira fought through it to pin the frantically struggling would-be murderer. "Fucking stay down," Mira warned.

It took forever, but it couldn't have been more than a few seconds, before Torin's reassuring voice penetrated her brain.

"It's okay, mo shearc. Laurents is here. We've got her. You can let go."

Her arms shook as she pushed herself off the brunette. She collapsed instantly, the adrenaline no longer supporting her.

She rolled onto her back, panting, not able to draw a breath.

"Take care of Araceli."

That was a woman's voice. *Inamorata?* Mira blinked, staring at the ceiling, unable to see anything. Panic unfurled in the pit of her stomach.

Torin stroked her forehead. She had no doubt it was him. No one else's touch reassured her like that.

"Hang tough, Araceli. An ambulance is on the way."

She tried to nod, and fresh pain rocketed her. "Sinclair?"

"Safe. Back at his hotel, no doubt."

"And the brunette?"

"You got her. Good job, Araceli." When he spoke again, his voice cracked. "Fucking exceptional."

Over the radio, Barstow spoke, his words breathless. "The unidentified blond male is on the move. Now out the back door. I'm in pursuit."

She pushed out a breath. "He's going to get away." All the man had to do was dodge into a bar, then out the rear entrance. "Goddamn it."

"The brunette is in custody," Torin reassured her. "We'll figure out the rest."

That wasn't good enough. They needed the blond man as well.

The frustration smacked up against her pain. Then her world went black.

When she was able to open her eyes again, the room spun. It took her long seconds to realize she was strapped onto a stretcher in the hotel ballroom. An IV drip ran into a vein, and Torin stood next to her, his jaw set in a brooding, frightening line.

"You scared the shit out of me, Araceli."

Her too.

Activity buzzed around her. New Orleans's finest officers were taking statements from those who'd been close enough to witness the events.

"We're going to need a statement," one of the policemen said.

"It can wait," Torin snapped.

"Sir—"

"Take it up the with the mayor if you need to. She's not talking to you until she's been seen by a doctor."

"But—"

Torin snarled. "Back off, Officer."

Inamorata showed up, as if by magic. "Our man, Laurents, saw the whole thing. I suggest you interview him."

Her words were a command, not a suggestion. No doubt she would call the mayor if necessary.

While their boss was occupied with the police, Torin took her hand.

Lines of anguish were trenched between his eyebrows.

"I'll be okay," she whispered. If it had been him who had been injured, how would she have reacted?

Their jobs came with risk, and they accepted that. In the lobby at Hawkeye's main headquarters near Denver, there was a glass wall etched with names of their compatriots who'd died in the line of duty. It was impossible to enter the offices or command center without walking past the silent, stark reminder of the danger every agent faced.

But what would she do if things had been reversed tonight?

Damn it. She loved him.

"We need to get her to the hospital," one of the paramedics said.

"I'm riding along," Torin said, voice holding no compromise.

"Nice work, Araceli," Inamorata said.

"Except for the part where she got shot," Torin countered.

Inamorata ignored him. "A commendation will go in your file."

"It was my job. Following my training." It was no small feat to teach someone to move toward danger instead of fleeing from it. "I had a good commander." She glanced at Torin. He didn't smile. In fact, his blue eyes chilled, reminding her of a glacier. The earlier concern had vanished. Now he was as remote as he had been when she was his student at Aiken.

The paramedics wheeled her from the ballroom, with Inamorata and Torin flanking the stretcher. "I want to exit through the rear entrance." She didn't want to be a focus or a spectacle.

Inamorata and Torin flanked the stretcher. "Already arranged," Inamorata assured her.

Outside, Torin climbed into the ambulance alongside her. "Commander Carter…"

His gaze was remote, and he didn't touch her. "We'll talk later."

She pressed her lips together. For the first time since her mother's death, tears threatened.

Something had happened in the ballroom, something she could never undo. It changed what was between them. "We—"

"Later, Araceli."

Her heart fractured at the harsh coldness in his tone.

"Barstow got his man," Inamorata said.

"Good." Normally, Torin would care. This morning, however, his thoughts were consumed with Araceli.

"Neither he nor the brunette are saying much. They lawyered up." She shrugged. "It's a job for the police now."

An uncomfortable silence hung between them. Narrowing his eyes, Torin stared across the kitchen table at his boss. Five minutes ago, she'd arrived at the carriage house, just as he was ready to leave for the hospital. "There's something you're not saying."

"I'm sending Araceli home."

"Home?"

"As in, we've placed her on medical leave. She needs to rest, and she isn't going to do it here. She'll want to work, and you know it."

Fuck.

"Hawkeye will be giving her a commendation. She did well."

He pushed back from the table to stalked the length of the living area. He stopped in front of a window and stared out, unseeingly "She got shot." *I could have lost her.* Though Mira hadn't required surgery, she faced weeks, if not months, of rehab before she could return to duty.

"You'll have a new partner in a couple of days, three at the most."

"What?" Barely restraining his sudden anger, he pivoted. "I need to be with her."

"That's not possible. With the Memorial Day weekend coming up, we need all the coverage that we can have."

"You're not separating us."

She raised one of her eyebrows. "Something I need to know, Commander Cater?"

Damnation. Was there? *Love.* Shit. He'd fallen in love with Araceli. He hadn't meant to fall in love with her. But from the beginning, there'd been an undeniable sexual attraction. She'd been too damn young, too innocent, and his student.

And now…?

She was a perfect sub. Still with something to prove.

"Is it possible you need some time, also?"

He snarled at his boss and fought for control over his fraying temper.

Mindless of the danger, much like Araceli, Inamorata continued. "After Ekaterina—"

"I'm warning you, Inamorata. Don't go there." A red haze blurred his vision.

"No?" She folded her arms over her cream-colored blazer. "How did you sleep last night?"

Unconsciously, he scrubbed a hand across his face.

More gently, she asked, "Did you sleep?"

He didn't need to answer.

The nightmare had been garish. But the reality of not knowing whether Mira was dead or alive—even for a few seconds—had been a thousand times more brutal. Blood was everywhere. And he'd stood there, paralyzed. Laurents pushed past Torin, and it had taken that jolt to make him move.

Now there were harsh truths to face.

"Risk is a hazard of the job. This is for Araceli's benefit. And yours. We need you, Commander, back at Aiken, but we need the best version of you that's possible. You're compromised…lost your edge."

She'd seen him freeze.

Inamorata was right.

Goddamn it to hell.

Ironic. When Araceli reported for training three years ago, he'd been concerned about her. In the end, he'd been the one to fail.

Inamorata stood. "One of our associates will be by in about an hour to collect her belongings."

"I'll pack them."

"That's not necessary."

"I said I'll do it." After she left, he slammed the door so hard it rattled in its casing.

Torin had always believed he was incapable of love and that his heart couldn't shatter. He was wrong.

CHAPTER NINE

HAWKEYE

"Let me get this straight…"

Torin looked across at Kayla Davidson Stone, the Hawkeye operative sent to replace Mira. Then he stopped to mentally correct himself. *To fill in for Mira.* No one could replace her, no matter how talented or determined.

The past few weeks had been the longest of his life.

He missed everything about Mira. Her secret smiles and stunningly submissive nature. He appreciated her wild abandon.

And, fuck it all, he even missed her feminine, wildflower scent.

When he packed up her things, he'd kept her bar of soap. Maybe a bit of a masochist himself, he'd left it in its porcelain dish where he was forced to look at it numerous times a day. Though the bar didn't really have a scent when it was dry, every time he showered, the moisture in the air seemed to release some of the fragrance, and it wrapped around him, reminding him of her. On one occasion, right after she left, the heady perfume had been so strong that he'd been convinced she'd returned.

He turned off the faucet and looked around. When she wasn't there, disappointment seared his lungs, making it impossible to breathe.

Kayla took a big bite of her beignet and grinned as powdered sugar flew everywhere.

"What?" He wrapped his hands around his cup of café au lait but didn't take a drink.

"You found a woman who could actually tolerate you."

"Excuse me?"

"I know. I couldn't believe it either when you told me."

Across the table on the banks of the Mississippi River, he glared at her.

"So, back to the conversation..."

"Can we talk about something other than my love life?"

"Like what? It's the only thing about you that isn't boring."

He'd known Kayla for years, and he'd worked with her on a couple of assignments. She'd recently settled down and she wanted to share her happiness with the rest of the world. It didn't seem to matter that he'd prefer she stuff her joy in a little bag and stow it out of sight.

He wasn't sure why the hell he'd told her anything about Mira. Well, except Kayla was curious about why she'd been summoned from Colorado to work with him.

This morning, around four, he'd awakened in a cold sweat, unable to move.

In his nightmares about Ekaterina, he relived the day he'd lost her. In the ones about Mira, she was very much alive, reaching out for him, and no matter what he did, he couldn't fight through the layer that separated them in order to touch her.

After escaping the tendrils of the horror slithering through his mind this morning, he'd gone for a run and then a swim before soaking in the hot tub.

Of course, when he returned to the carriage house, Kayla had questions, and she'd relentlessly assaulted him with them until he agreed to talk. In that way, she was a lot like Araceli.

"Are you listening to me?" Kayla snapped her fingers in front of his face.

He shook his head.

"I was asking why you let her go." She popped the rest of the French-style donut in her mouth.

He closed his jaw so fast that his back teeth smacked together. "I didn't fucking let her go."

"Did you tell Inamorata to go to hell? Get lost?"

Putting down his cup, he regarded Kayla.

She brushed her hands together. "When Wolf decided he wanted me and Nate, he prepared letters of resignation for all of us. He told Hawkeye the terms of our continued employment, and we were all willing to walk away unless we got what we wanted. Which was each other."

"It's not that easy."

"Oh. Cuz you're special, Commander?"

"I'm returning to Aiken next month." After a solo vacation.

"And Mira?"

He shrugged while Kayla reached for a second pastry. When they placed their order, they'd agreed to share. But she was showing no signs of moving the plate to the middle of the table.

"Do you love her?"

"What the hell does that have to do with anything?" He drank half of his rapidly cooling café au lait.

Very much unlike her, she watched him in silence.

Finally, he fractured. His voice cracked with emotion as he spoke. "I froze."

"You were scared." Her tone was matter-of-fact. "That's human. I can't imagine coping if either Nate or Stone were to be wounded. But we can't let our fear get in the way of living our lives. We savor each day, maybe even more than we might otherwise, because we don't know if it will be our last."

That wasn't the way he wanted to live. Maybe he wasn't even capable of it.

"Love makes cowards of us all, Commander Carter. It's up to you what you do with that fear." She covered his hand with hers. "You may always have the nightmares. I wonder…"

He waited for her to go on. No doubt, she would.

"Not knowing where Mira is, what's she doing—will that make the future easier for you?" She released him to snatch the last beignet.

He knew the answer to that.

After he started sleeping with Araceli in his bed, curled next to him, his nightmares had abated. Now that she was gone, they were worse than ever.

"Only you can make your decisions. If I were you, I'd confront my fears. Because in the darkness, they grow."

The words haunted him long past the time they returned to the carriage house. As afternoon gave way to evening, he considered going to the Quarter.

Just as he had the past ten times he thought about it, he dismissed the idea. Araceli had ruined him for other subs. He didn't want to scene with anyone other than her. And for the first time, he had no interest in observing others.

In the darkest part of the night, he realized there was only one possible way out of this despair. He had to move through it. Acknowledge his weaknesses. Only then could he find the courage to face the risks that came with loving Araceli.

"So, I've been dying to ask…"

Mira stirred her rum punch with the tiny pink umbrella

the bartender had placed in it. Dreading the question, she glanced at Hallie. More than ever, she was grateful for the support and help of her friend. For the past two weekends, Hallie had driven to Mira's place in Covington, on the north shore of Lake Pontchartrain. Not only that, but she'd stayed, done some cooking, helped with the housework, and most of all, alleviated some of Mira's constant boredom.

In her entire life, she'd never been out of commission for more than a day. Two at the most. Being incapacitated was worse than she'd ever imagined. She was lonely. And worse, she couldn't turn her mind off.

Every day, she replayed the events of the time she'd spent with Torin.

Because she and Hallie were at a loud casual restaurant filled with other Saturday night partiers, Hallie had to shout to be heard. "Have you heard from Master Hottie?"

Mira exhaled a weighty sigh. "No."

Hallie sat back, taking her wineglass with her. "I don't get it."

After regaining consciousness the night she'd been shot, Mira had seen bleakness in Torin's eyes and known something had changed.

Had he been thinking about Ekaterina? Drowning in memories?

In response to Mira's questions, Inamorata had been vague, merely saying that Torin was required to finish up his assignment in New Orleans.

She'd then secured Mira's release from the hospital and sent her on her way in a limo. Since then, Hawkeye had arranged for follow-up doctor's visits, provided all the HR paperwork to ensure she received her pay without interruption. Even though she protested that it wasn't necessary, they'd provided meal delivery and a driver for two weeks.

Even when her mother passed, Mira hadn't cried.

Since she left New Orleans, she hadn't stopped.

Hallie took a drink, then looked at Mira with a frown. "That night at the Quarter, he seemed like he was really into you."

Mira wasn't sure how to respond. He was. Obviously, that wasn't enough.

Hallie's eyes lit up, and she put down her glass. "You should call him!"

"Not on your life."

"Why not?"

She swirled her umbrella around and around. "Would you?" Mira countered.

"I think so." Hallie nodded.

"Really?"

"I think so. Yes. At least get some closure? Right?"

The server delivered a huge plate of nachos—Mira's favorite comfort food. Salt and warm melty cheese, with plenty of crunch. Tomorrow, she'd add a walk, maybe a short run, to her rehab program.

"Enough about me." Mira transferred a few chips onto her plate. "How're things with Master Bartholomew?"

"Well..." Hallie grinned. "Amazing. We played last night at the Quarter, and he stayed overnight. Evidently Bartholomew is his last name."

Evidently? Meaning Hallie believed so but wasn't certain?

"And yes. Before you start with your dozens of questions, he's willing to meet you. As soon as you're up for it, the three of us can go out to dinner or something."

"I want a full name."

"So you can do your spy shit?" She shook her head.

"At least give me a name."

"Nope." Hallie stabbed her fork into a jalapeno pepper. "Not happening."

"Hallie..."

"You can't give it a rest, can you?"

Mira sighed. "Of course I can. Yes."

"Tell me about the couple who just got seated."

Without glancing away, Mira replied. "They've been married about ten years, give or take. Probably a couple of kids at home. Date night. Headed to the movies after dinner. Need to get back for the babysitter by eleven."

Hallie laughed. "It couldn't be a first date?"

"Nah. They both look exhausted. Besides, he'd take her somewhere they could talk more intimately."

"I rest my case!" Hallie bit into a chip while Mira frowned

At the end of the evening, they exchanged quick hugs in the parking lot. "Call him."

"I just need to get on with my life." There was no sense in mourning a brief fling with her former instructor. *Right?* Clearly, he was not wasting any time thinking about her. Mira shook her head. "I want to meet Master Bartholomew. Let me know what day works out for you? I can meet any day next week." She needed something on the calendar to look forward to. And poking around in Hallie's life was much more appealing than worrying about her own.

"I'll let you know."

When she was back in the car, Mira pulled her phone out of her purse.

There were no missed calls. No text messages. No emails.

Even though she hadn't expected anything different, she dropped her head onto the steering wheel as her heart splintered all over again.

CHAPTER TEN

HAWKEYE

A gunshot shredded the air. Eyes wide, reaching for him, Araceli crumpled, her blood dripping onto the white marble floor. He reached for her, and she vanished like a specter. "No!" His scream ricocheted through the room, horrifyingly useless.

In terror, he jolted awake.

Heart thundering so hard that it echoed in his ears, Torin gulped in a breath.

Shit.

The dreams were no longer random or rare occurrences. Since he'd left Araceli, they were constant and unwelcome companions.

Minutes later, when his pulse was close to normal, he crawled from the bed and headed outside.

He had no idea how many laps he'd put in, but when he hauled himself out of the swimming pool and dropped, exhausted, into a chair in the courtyard, the future was so clear that he was unsure how he hadn't recognized it before.

Mira was *his.* His to protect. To dominate.

Without her, the future loomed long and bleak, an

endless series of new recruits and lonely nights at Hawkeye's Nevada compound.

Facing his fear was easier than facing a future without her.

He needed her.

Torin sluiced water from his face.

Kayla walked down the stairs, carrying a bottle of water and mug. Without an invitation, she sat down across from him and placed the coffee in front of him.

Gratefully, he took a long drink of the thick, dark brew. "I'm going to take the rest of the day off."

"Good. I want to go and do some shopping, anyway." She picked at the label on her bottle. "New clothes."

He narrowed his eyes. No caffeine. A second order of beignets when they'd been at Café du Monde... "Are..." He proceeded with care. "Congratulations in order?"

"It's secret." She grinned. "And brand-new news. I just came here to help you get your head on straight, and then I'll be transferring to Ops for the foreseeable future

"You—"

"Inamorata and Hawkeye wanted to give you time to get past the shooting, find your footing. They figured you would refuse to take time off. And they guessed you wouldn't be sleeping."

He blinked. He and Kayla had been given relatively few assignments, and none of them involved anything dangerous. *"Fuck."*

"Are you going after your woman, Commander Carter?"

His woman. He liked the sound of that. "Yeah."

She tipped her water bottle in his direction, and he headed back upstairs.

Torin could send her a text message, but he dismissed that idea as too casual. A phone call wouldn't work either. It would be far too easy for her to send him to voicemail. Even if she answered, that wouldn't be enough for him. He wanted to read her expression, look into her eyes to see the things she wanted to hide. If he was lucky enough, touch her.

Since he didn't know where she lived, he contacted Hawkeye headquarters. Not surprisingly, they denied his request for information. Next, he tried a couple of operatives and an IT guru, all of whom owed him favors. No one agreed to help.

Which left him with old-fashioned search options. He thought she had a house in Louisiana, so he began there.

Annoying the hell out of him, it took hours, much longer than it should have. Of course, Hawkeye had buried her information under several layers of security.

Once he'd programmed her address into his GPS, he sat in his vehicle for a few minutes, wondering whether she'd actually be there or not. She could be anywhere on the planet, on vacation, even on an assignment if she'd skipped out on rehab and returned to duty.

There was also the very real possibility she might not want to see him.

Still, he had to see her again. Then he would deal with the ramifications.

A LEMONADE IN FRONT OF HER, MIRA SAT IN THE WHITE wicker swing on her front porch. An overhead fan churned through the humid air but did little to dissipate June's cloying heat.

She was restless, anxious to return to work. This morning, the physical therapist said she'd be cleared for duty in another week, perhaps two.

But she was tired of television, books, magazines, online shopping, and especially her thoughts. Hallie had invited her to the Quarter, but the risk of seeing Torin was too high, and Mira wasn't strong enough for that. If he was with another submissive...

Damn. Getting involved with Torin *had* been stupid.

Mira hated that their relationship now meant she didn't want to visit her favorite club.

She took a drink from the overly tart lemonade, then rolled the glass across her forehead. Maybe she should invite Hallie and Bartholomew over for dinner this weekend. And in the meantime, maybe Mira could begin a little surreptitious research on the man. Spy shit would be a welcome distraction.

A vehicle turned onto the street.

This was what her life had been reduced to. Watching the comings and goings, wondering what was in the packages delivered by a big brown truck.

The SUV passed a couple of houses.

Her heart lurched as she saw the color of the car. Gloss white. *Like Torin's.*

Warning herself to stop the fantastical thinking, Mira slid her glass onto a nearby table. She couldn't conjure Torin. He didn't know where she lived, and there was no way Hawkeye would divulge her whereabouts.

The vehicle crawled forward, as if the driver wasn't sure exactly where to stop.

Her pulse picked up, despite the urgings of her left brain. There were hundreds, if not thousands, of gloss-white SUVs in Covington. This particular one meant nothing, no matter how much she wanted it to belong to Torin.

Two houses away, the driver parked alongside the curb.

Annoyed with herself for even the momentary lapse of judgement, she snatched up the glass and took a long drink.

The engine fell silent, leaving a mockingbird as the only sound.

She leaned forward for a peek, telling herself she was looking out for her neighbors, making sure things were safe while they were at work.

A man emerged, and her view was obscured by an oversize live oak tree. He had stark raven-black hair that was slightly too long.

Despite the temperature, Mira shivered.

Of course he would park down the street to allow himself time to assess the situation. *Spy shit.*

For several seconds, she considered what to do.

Go inside? Turn the dead bolt? Maybe feign surprise when she opened the door. Perhaps—to protect herself—she should ignore him entirely.

That was her preferred option, and the only one she was incapable of.

She remained where she was, threading her fingers into the material of her skirt. Then, realizing that was a betrayal of her nerves, she stood.

As he passed the magnolia tree, she studied the beautiful, harsh planes of his face. Breath vanished from her lungs.

The moment he noticed her, he stopped.

Even across the distance, she saw the worry lines trenched deeply next to his blue eyes. Torin had aged a decade since that night in the hospital.

She had no doubt he hadn't been sleeping.

Slowly he continued toward her, turning onto the path, then stopping at the bottom of the porch stairs. "I…"

Her confident, fearless former instructor ran a finger between his black T-shirt and his nape.

Because she didn't know why he was here and was too damn scared to guess, she remained where she was, saying nothing.

"I…" He took a breath.

Hurt and confusion left her unable to speak or act.

"May I...?" Torin swept his hand in front of him, indicating the stairs, the distance separating them.

Don't be here to break my heart.

He cleared his throat. "I fucked up."

Of all the words she'd dreamed of, those hadn't been among them.

"I came to apologize."

Saying nothing, she stroked a thumb across her index finger.

"I need to see how you are."

"I'm fine."

"You're pissed." He smiled, but it was the barest hint of one, and it faded fast.

Time stretched. A mockingbird zipped overhead to land in a nearby tree. The fan continued to churn.

"The truth is..."

Tears stung her eyes. Again. What was it about this man that brought emotion out in her?

"Seeing you hurt devastated me. I froze. When you blacked out, Laurents knocked me out of the way to get to you. I'm not proud. But there it is. I've never been paralyzed by fear before."

"I wasn't seriously injured."

"Logically." He shrugged. "Tell that to my heart."

She couldn't help herself. "You have one?"

Torin winced. "I deserve that."

Struggling to hide her vulnerability, she clamped her lips together.

"May I please come up the stairs?"

"If you've said what you came here for, there's no need." She had to send him away before she begged him to stay.

"Damn it, Araceli." His voice cracked. "This wasn't how this was supposed to go."

His hand trembled. Stunned, she moved her gaze to his.

"I'm screwing this up. What I mean to say is…I love you."

She blinked. It wasn't possible that she'd heard him right. "You…?"

"I love you," he repeated, voice more confident. "You can tell me to go to hell. I wouldn't blame you. But I couldn't live the rest of my life without telling you." He paused. "And asking forgiveness. I don't deserve that, God knows. And I don't expect anything from you. Tell me to get in the car and leave you the hell alone. But for the love of all things holy, say *something*."

The breath she hadn't realized she'd taken seared her lungs. Slowly, she released it. Her legs wobbled. She loved him. The crush she'd had during training had matured into something strong enough to withstand the ache of despair and the revelation of his deepest human failings.

His stark emotion melted her heart into a pool of compassion.

He was a man who needed her love to survive.

Not trusting her voice, she stepped to one side in silent invitation.

He took the two steps with great deliberation.

Now that he was close, her senses swam. His scent, of masculine determination and a moonlit night, was welcoming, inviting her home. She could more clearly read his eyes and the tiny sparks of grief in them.

"Nightmares?" she managed.

"Every time I try to sleep."

He lifted a hand as if to touch her, then dropped it to his side, perhaps realizing that spoke of an intimacy they no longer shared. "Not about Ekaterina." Pain haunted his words. "That's not why I'm here. I can deal with that." He shrugged, but it was a halfhearted attempt. "I had to come. It's selfish, maybe. Probably. But I needed to see you, look in your eyes, hear you tell me to go away. If you do, I'll respect your wishes."

The words hung between them.

"Actually. No. I won't. That's a fucking lie." He grinned ruefully and plowed a hand into his hair. "I'm going to spend the rest of my life telling you I love you and trying to make up for this. For letting fear paralyze me. For being an asshole."

The instinct for self-preservation deserted her. He was capable of hurting her more than any other person ever had, yet she couldn't tell him to leave. Every part of her craved him. "Tell me again."

He swallowed. "That I love you?"

"No." A damn tear spilled from the corner of her eye. "How bad you fucked up."

"Totally."

She swiped a hand across her face. "Completely."

"One hundred percent. Jerk."

"That'll suffice. Now tell me the other stuff again." It was all she could do not to launch herself into his arms.

"I love you, Araceli." He quirked an eyebrow. "That part?"

"You're getting there."

"I'll spend my life trying to make it up to you."

"That's better."

"I... Damn it, Araceli. If you're going to forgive me, put me out of my misery. Please?"

She took a step toward him. And that was all her Dominant lover needed. He closed the remaining distance and gently drew her toward him. "How's your arm?"

"It was superficial. I'm almost done with rehab."

"Do you love me? No. Wait." He shook his head. "You don't have to say anything. I'll be the man you deserve until you fall in love with me."

She looked at him without blinking, allowing him to see

her all of her, holding nothing back, the tears, the anguish, the depth of her emotion. "I think I fell in love with you at Aiken. I've never stopped."

"You...?"

"Yes. I love you, Torin."

The breath he released was jagged, as if dragged across the shards of his heart. "I've missed you."

She traced a finger across one of his eyebrows. Because of the vulnerability in his tone, she offered her own confession. "It's mutual, Commander Carter."

"We have a lot of talking to do."

"About?"

"The future. Marriage. How we'll make this—Hawkeye—work. Or not. Nothing, nothing is more important than being with you. If you want me to resign, I will. I don't know what we'll do, but as long as it's together, we can figure it out. Nothing is more important to me, Mira, than being with you."

"Marriage?" Of all the things he'd said, it was the only thing she'd heard.

"Maybe kids."

She swallowed hard. "What?"

"Long story. Kayla Davidson Stone is pregnant. And I started thinking."

"Kiss me?"

He did, with care and a gentleness she'd never experienced from him. "I'm not fragile."

"But you are precious." He brushed back strands of her hair, then framed her face with his hands before leaning in to give her a kiss that tasted of the promise of a thousand tomorrows.

Her toes curled, and sexual arousal rushed through her, leaving her dizzy. Desperate, she grabbed his forearms for support.

Just then, a hoot and raucous clapping snapped through her reverie. Theodore, her nosy retired next door neighbor, leaned on his porch rail, grinning.

Embarrassment flooded her. No doubt she would be the talk of his breakfast club the next morning. "I'm so sorry you saw that, Mr. Winters!"

"It's about time you stopped moping around, Mira."

"Moping?" Torin raised an eyebrow.

She rolled her eyes but gave her neighbor a half smile.

"We're getting married," Torin called out.

"Darn right you are," Mr. Winters shouted back. "Otherwise I'm going to get my shotgun."

"You didn't propose," she pointed out in a fierce whisper. "And I haven't agreed."

"You will."

Once again, she was engulfed by the sweet relentless storm that was Torin Carter.

"I think we should go inside," Torin said. "You definitely don't want him to see what I've got planned for you next."

"Oh?"

He swept her from her feet, and she placed a hand around his neck for stability.

"We have some time to make up for. And I plan to start doing that right away."

HAWKEYE

"We're going to need a different ladder," Mira said, looking up at the Christmas tree that stood over fourteen feet tall.

"We're going to need scaffolding," Torin corrected, coming up behind her to slide his arms possessively around her waist. "A crane, maybe. That is, if you still want the star on top."

She maneuvered herself around to face him. "It needs it."

"How do you know? No one can see the top."

Mira raised her eyebrows.

Her husband of three months sighed. "I figured it was worth a try." Then a sly grin sauntered across his features, sending her insides into a freefall. "It will cost you."

His eyes glittered with Dominant intent, and she was more than willing to pay his price. "You have to admit, the tree is perfect."

"Better than I imagined."

Once Mira agreed to marry him, Torin hadn't been content to wait, and they'd spent a few days away, on vacation, making plans for their future.

Since neither of them wanted to quit working for Hawkeye Security and they wanted to be together as much as possible, she'd applied for a teaching position at Aiken Training Facility.

Once she was offered the job, she and Torin started house hunting, spending hours a day poring through pictures online.

She'd fallen in love with the large space, designed to resemble a log cabin. The main living area had a soaring cathedral ceiling and numerous skylights, meaning the interior would be flooded with light even during the long northern Nevada winters.

Torin had urged her toward caution. The home needed extensive renovations, and it was impossible to tell how sound it was until they had it inspected.

But the moment they walked in the front door, the space wrapped around her, seeming to welcome her home.

Torin had been more skeptical, until their real estate agent showed them a secret room behind a bookcase in the master bedroom.

Suddenly he, too, had seen the property's potential.

"Spy shit," Hallie had said when Mira told her about it. "Of course you'd love it."

From the moment they hired the contractors, she'd known it was the perfect spot for them to build their new life together. They were on several acres of land. They were close enough to work that the commute wasn't terrible, and far enough away to have privacy after they left the training facility.

"I'll take payment in advance," he informed her.

"Will you, Commander Carter?"

All traces of teasing vanished from his eyes. "Master Torin."

Instantly she slid into a submissive mindset. If he hadn't been holding her, she would have knelt.

"I'll meet you in the play room."

Even though they'd been lovers for over six months, when his tone was roughened with dominant demand, her mouth dried, making words almost impossible.

"Fifteen minutes?"

She nodded.

"Please wear a thong, fishnet stockings, a garter belt, and heels."

Slowly, he released her. "Don't be late, mo shearc."

She hurried up the stairs, and on the landing, turned to look down at him. Arms folded across his long-sleeved Henley T-shirt, he was watching her.

"You're down to fourteen minutes, sub."

"Sir." She hurried into their bedroom and pulled open the drawer of her closed built-in. One of the stockings snagged on a leather bra clasp, increasing her sense of urgency. The faster she moved, the slower she seemed to go.

In every area of her life, she was more than competent, but when it came to scening with him, she couldn't keep her thoughts straight.

She selected a red garter belt and a black thong as her mind spun through a dozen different possibilities. The Saint Andrew's cross? The spanking bench? Or the Wall of Torture designed by a friend of his in Denver?

The panties slipped from her trembling fingers.

That was her favorite thing, and he was incredibly inventive when it came to using the numerous metal rails attached to wall.

In the near distance, the door to their bedroom opened, which meant Torin had entered and her time might be running short.

She forced herself to take a few deep breaths before stripping.

Even thought the heater had cycled recently, her nipples became hardened little beads. And they ached for his attention.

Two minutes later, she slipped into her highest heels, then walked through their bedroom and into the secret room.

Torin was in the center of the room, an acrylic paddle strapped to his side.

In the doorway, she hesitated. She hated the thing as much as she loved it. It was brutal, but each time she took it, she adored the resulting endorphins.

Though she had made peace with her need to push herself to achieve ever-greater results, she still enjoyed being taken to her limits. And it was astounding to know that he was there for her, always watching and caring.

"Oh, Mira..." He drew a breath, and his eyes became hooded as he swept his gaze over her. "Even more beautiful than this morning."

At dawn, he'd made sweet love to her, and he'd listed a dozen things he cherished about her. His constant appreciation nourished her on a soul-deep level, making her wonder how she'd managed without him.

"Please come to me."

Her shoes echoed off the hardwood flooring, the strike matching her heartbeat.

"What is tonight about?" he asked when she was in front of him.

Her tender lover from earlier had been replaced by this badass Dom.

"I want a favor from you..." She hesitated. Lowering her gaze, she finished. "Sir."

He groaned. "You're the perfect sub."

She looked up at him through her lashes.

"Your nipples are already hard."

In a fraction of a second, he'd once again become her Master.

"Perhaps you're anticipating having them clamped?"

Her pussy dampened.

"I didn't hear you."

"Anything you want, Sir."

"That's what I thought. Please put your hands behind your neck."

Obediently, she did as he said. He grabbed the front of her thong and pulled forward and up, forcing her onto her toes. She gasped. Mira had been sure he was going to play with her breasts, so this unexpected move hit her with double force.

The material split her in half and seared her clit.

She hissed out a breath.

"I love hurting you like this."

His grip, combined with the power of his words, sent a climax crashing through her.

"You didn't come, did you?" He made a small *tsking* sound.

"I'm sorry, Sir."

"Don't worry about apologizing."

He was a devil of a Dom. He'd work hard to give her an orgasm, then punish her for it.

No wonder she was addicted to him.

"Now your nipples." Torin released her thong but left the material scrunched uncomfortably in her crotch. He rolled each nipple, tweaking, squeezing, tugging until she was breathless and it took all of her self-control to remain in the position he'd ordered.

Then without warning, he sucked one into his mouth, applying harsh pressure and a tiny bite.

"Oh, Sir!"

With a horrid chuckle, he moved on to the other side, sucking until she cried his name over and over.

Without warning, he left her to select a pair of Japanese clover clamps from a drawer in the armoire he'd had built to hold their toys.

This pair had an extralong chain between them, which meant awful things for her.

Involuntarily, she shivered.

It'd been a while since they had a scene this intense. Until her whole body throbbed, she hadn't realized how badly she needed it.

He placed the clamps, then gave them a sharp tug, making her yelp.

"That didn't sound like a safe word."

"It wasn't, Sir," she assured him.

"I want you at the wall, wife."

Yes. *Yes, please.*

"But first…"

Puzzled, she looked at him.

He pulled out a pair of weights from a back pocket.

In order not to protest, she clamped her lips together. Those things would be horribly uncomfortable.

The pain-loving submissive in her soared as he wrapped her chain around one of his hands, holding it steady while he affixed the hefty teardrop-shaped pieces of metal in place.

"Should I gently let go? Or should I drop it so it yanks on you?"

They both knew it wasn't her decision. His questions were meant to stoke her fear.

"Naughty girl that you are, you'd come again if I did that." He leaned toward her and kissed her forehead. "Wouldn't you?"

"I…"

He dropped the chain. She cried out from the sudden shock. Between her legs, the weights swung back and forth.

She closed her eyes against the pain.

As always, he knew what she needed, and he stroked a thumb between her legs, vanquishing everything except pleasure.

"Don't you dare even consider coming."

Mira floated somewhere ethereal, where nothing existed but the moment and her man.

"Let's get you to the wall."

With his arms folded, he watched her. Each step made the weights sway, forcing her to take slow, small steps.

She hazarded a glance Torin's direction. His cock bulged against his jeans. His arousal was reward enough for her suffering.

A little more than a foot from the wall, he instructed her to stop. "Please bend over and extend your arms forward. And your feet should never cross that line."

Now she knew why he'd placed a strip of blue tape on the floor.

About waist height, he secured her wrists in place. Her back was flat, and the weights were only a couple of inches off the floor. Her bonds would prevent her from standing, and any movement would make her nipples ache.

"Comfortable?"

"Not in the least, Sir."

"Ah. In that case, let's consider it perfect."

Mira might have guessed he'd say that.

After caressing her shoulders—with a gentleness that contrasted powerfully with his sternness—he left her for a few seconds and then returned to stroke between her legs. She fought to keep still, but with the way she was already aroused, it was beyond difficult.

Despite her best intentions, she moved, trying to entice

him to stroke her clit harder. He brushed aside her thong to insert a finger in her pussy. "Oh, Sir!"

"You may orgasm. But each time you do, I'll add four strokes to your paddling."

"That's madness, Sir!"

"To the contrary, my darling bride. You're in complete control. We'll start with the eight I want to give you, and we'll go as high as you wish." Without warning, he dug his fingers into one of her buttocks and separated it from the other in order to more easily press a cold, slick plug into her anus.

"Ugh!" This was bigger than the one he usually used on her, making her struggle until she managed to control her breathing.

Torin had never demanded this much from her before, and she adored him all the more for it. He knew what drove her.

When she settled in, breathing hard to fight off an orgasm, he slipped a U-shaped vibrator into her pussy and turned it on, filling her with a slow occasional pulse.

After her first whimper, he placed the gusset of her thong over the tiny toy to hold it in.

Not knowing what to expect or when made it all the more difficult to control her reactions.

He stepped back, then used the remote control to turn up the device's intensity.

Panting for breath, Mira squirmed, trying to escape while being unyieldingly held in place.

"We're starting with eight strikes from the paddle."

The thing was a beast. Though it was much thinner than some of her wooden paddles, it hurt significantly worse. It had a little give, and if he pulled it back right away, its burn would be more significant.

Always the perfect Dominant, he warmed her up, delivering a few spanks with his hand. Because of the way the vibrator danced in her and the plug filled her ass, another orgasm was already forming.

She wanted to get this over with. "Sir..."

He stopped spanking her to fuck her with the toy.

Damn. No. No. "No!" The orgasm plowed into her. Arching her back, she tugged against her restraints, swinging the weights attached to her clamps.

Mira was miserable and now had to take extra strokes.

"How many orgasms since we started?"

Before answering, she hesitated. "Two, but... Well, that first one... You hadn't said I'd receive four more spanks for that one."

"I see. So you want more?"

"No! Sir." How did he always do this to her? Tie up her thoughts as surely as her body?

"Count them for me."

He delivered the first six in a precise and measured way, making them as easy to take as possible.

After the seventh, he squeezed her right nipple.

In a useless, desperate attempt to escape, she bent her knees.

"Where are we?" he asked, even though she knew he hadn't forgotten. He'd never be that careless.

"Seven. Sir."

"Meaning?"

"Five more."

He gave her another two before squeezing her left nipple. As she sidled away, he delivered two more spanks, and the sensations overcame her, pushing her over the edge again.

"Oh dear." Pleasure was threaded through his words, letting her know how much he enjoyed paddling her. "Now how many?"

From her position, the spanks, the orgasms, and the relentless whir of the vibrator, the world was turning pink.

"Seven. Sir."

She was aware of the next two, then… Nothing. Just an empty, peaceful void, where she floated.

"Mira?"

Pain shot through her nipples. Then it was instantly eased as he squeezed each of them.

"Are you back?"

She blinked. Subspace? One of his arms was beneath her belly, supporting her upper body.

Then her wrists were free, and he was making broad circles on her skin to help restore circulation. She wouldn't have noticed if he hadn't since every part of her felt warm and wonderful.

Torin carried her back to the bedroom and then used a warm, damp cloth to bathe her after he removed the plug and the vibrator.

Tucked beneath the covers, in her husband's arms, Mira continued to drift.

She had no idea how long it took her to become aware of reality again, and when she did, Torin was smiling at her.

"We need to do that more often."

"Yes. Please." Scening was an amazing stress relief, and it also reconnected them. For a couple of months after she was wounded, he'd been afraid of hurting her and had refused to play with her at all. The connection, when he finally relented, had cemented their relationship as nothing else could.

Since they'd been in their home, his nightmares had stopped, and she'd let down her guard for the first time in her life.

Outside their window, the sun yielded to night. "I heard back from Hallie this afternoon," she said.

"Oh?" He moved his head so he could look at her as she

spoke.

"She and Bartholomew are going to come and stay for a few days around New Year."

"Good."

Since he knew she missed her friend, he'd been the one to suggest the visit. That would give them a few weeks to finish the renovations on the guest apartment above their three-car garage.

"Did you ever do a background check on him?"

"Hallie asked me not to. Remember?"

"I noticed you didn't answer the question. Which is your way of fibbing without actually lying."

"Maybe a quick search for a criminal record."

"Mira…"

That was fair. She'd stopped short of going through his finances. "But someone named Bartholomew is automatically suspect. It's fancy, right? Like a rich name. Or a fake one."

"It's been eight months, right? If there were warning signs, you'd have seen them by now."

She wondered. It'd taken Hallie's ex-boyfriend a year to reveal his.

"Hallie's happy with him."

Which should be enough.

"She's right that you should give the spy shit a rest."

With a small smile, she snuggled back into his arms.

"I'm going to make love to you, Mira."

Happier than she had a right to be, she pulled back the blankets.

Torin stroked his fingers into her hair, then tugged back her head and held it still as he lowered his mouth to hers with purposeful intent. "You were meant for me. And I will never let you go."

Mira shivered from the husky intensity in his voice. "You

are the only man I have ever loved. I've never wanted anyone but you." The she sighed, surrendering to his deep, all-consuming kiss.

◊ ◊ ◊ ◊ ◊

Thank you for reading Meant For Me. I hope you enjoyed Mira and Torin's love story. I invite you to spend time with another Hawkeye agent, the irresistible Jacob Walker in Hold On To Me. He is supposed to protect her, not fall in love.

Cowboy and former military operative Jacob Walker can't refuse one last mission, protecting the beautiful, fiery Elissa. But she refuses to be whisked away from her life like a terrified damsel in distress. But that's exactly what happens when she finds herself thrown over the muscular shoulder of one very inflexible, annoying, and handsome, alpha bodyguard. Once she's at his remote ranch she discovers something much more dangerous than the threat facing her—her very real attraction to her smoking-hot captor.

DISCOVER HOLD ON TO ME

If you enjoyed Torin and Mira's trip to the Quarter in New Orleans, you'll love His to Claim. It was only supposed to be for a weekend. Now the overwhelming billionaire Dominant is demanding Hannah's heart forever.

★★★★★ Full of real, raw, beautiful emotions with vibrant characters. ~*Amazon Reviewer*

DISCOVER HIS TO CLAIM

Turn the page for an exciting excerpt from Hold On To Me.

HOLD ON TO ME
CHAPTER ONE EXCERPT

"No fucking way, Hawkeye." In case that wasn't clear enough, Jacob Walker tipped back the brim of his cowboy hat and leveled a stare at his friend and former commander across the small, rickety table that separated them.

The stench of cheap whiskey and loneliness hung in the air—as putrid as it was familiar.

Through the years, they'd held dozens of meetings at this kind of place. Didn't matter which fucked-up hellhole they were in—Central America, the Middle East, Texas, or here, a small, all but forgotten Colorado mountain town, a place with no security cameras, where neither of them were known.

As usual, Hawkeye dressed to blend in with the locals—jeans, scuffed boots, and a heavyweight canvas jacket that could be found on almost every ranch in the state. He'd added a baseball cap with a logo of a tractor company embroidered on the front. Today, he also wore a beard. No doubt it would be gone within an hour of his walking back outside into the crisp, clean air.

At one time, Jacob thrived on clandestine meetings. The anticipation alone was enough to feed adrenaline into his veins, and he lived for the vicarious thrill.

But life was different now.

After a final, fateful job in Colombia that left an American businessman's daughter dead, Jacob walked away from Hawkeye Security.

He returned to the family ranch and a world he no longer recognized. His grandfather had died, no doubt from the stress of managing the holdings by himself. Though Jacob's grandmother never uttered a critical word, he knew she was disappointed that he'd missed the funeral. He wasn't even in the same country when he was needed the most.

When she passed, he stood alone at the graveside, the only family mourner, like she'd no doubt been a few years before.

Spurred by equal measures of guilt and regret, he poured himself into managing the family's holdings as a way to redeem himself. Then, because of his loneliness and the horrible dreams after Colombia, he did it as a way to save himself.

"The op will take less than a month." Hawkeye shrugged. "Give or take. I'll give you three of our best agents—Johnson, Laurents, Mansfield. You can man the gate, rather than just utilizing the speaker box. Another on perimeter. One for relief. You have the space and a bunkhouse."

Jacob shook his head to clear it of the ever-present memories. "Is there a part of my refusal that you don't understand?" Of course there was. When Hawkeye wanted something, nothing would dissuade him. That willful determination had made him a force on the battlefield as well as in the business arena. "When I quit, I meant it." He took a swig from his longneck beer bottle. "No regrets." The words were mostly true. There were times he wanted the camaraderie and wanted to flex his brain as well as his muscles. There was also the sweet thrill of the hunt. And making things right in the world.

Rather than argue, Hawkeye removed his cap long enough for Jacob to get a look at his former boss. Worry lines were trenched between his eyebrows. In all his years, Jacob had never seen dark despair in those eyes. "Yesterday, Inamorata received what appeared to be a birthday card from her sister."

Ms. Inamorata was Hawkeye's right-hand woman and known for her ability to remain calm under duress. She could be counted on to deal with local and federal authorities, smoothing over all the details. Rather seriously, Hawkeye said she batted cleanup better than any major leaguer.

Jacob told himself to stand up, thank Hawkeye for the drink, then get the hell out of here while he still could. Instead, he remained where he was.

"There was a white powder inside."

Jesus. "Anthrax?"

"Being tested. She took appropriate precautions and received immediate medical assistance. Antibiotics were prescribed as a precaution." Hawkeye paused. "There were no warning signs that the piece of mail was suspicious."

Meaning the postmark matched the return address. The postage amount was correct, and there was nothing protruding from the envelope.

Jacob knew Inamorata and liked her as much as he respected her. He took offense at a threat to her life. "Received at headquarters?"

"No. At her home. So whoever sent it has access to information about her and how to circumvent our protocols."

Slowly he nodded. "Any message?"

171

"Yeah." Hawkeye paused. "Threats to take out people I care about, one at a time."

"The fuck?" Instead of sympathizing, Jacob switched to ops mode. He didn't do it on purpose—it was as immediate as it was instinctive. No doubt Hawkeye had counted on Jacob's reaction. "Anything else?"

"There was no specific request. No signature." Hawkeye paused. "I've got profilers taking a look at it. But there's not much to go on. Tech is analyzing writing and sentence structure, tracking down places the card could have come from. FBI has the powder at its lab. Profilers are trying to ascertain the type of person most likely to behave this way."

All the right things.

"But we don't have the resources to take care of our clients and have eyes on everyone who's a potential target."

At this point, there was no way to know how serious the threat was. A card was one thing, a physical attack was another.

"I don't give a fuck who comes for me."

Over the years, their line of work—cleaning up situations to keep secrets safe, protecting people and precious objects, even acting as paramilitary support operators overseas—had created a long list of enemies.

"But I can't risk the people I care about." Hawkeye reached into a pocket inside his jacket and pulled out a picture. "I need you to take care of her."

"Oh fuck no, man." Jacob could be a sounding board, analyze data, but he didn't have the time to return to babysitting services.

Undeterred, Hawkeye continued. "Her name's Elissa. Elissa Conroy. Twenty-eight. My plan was to have Agent Fagen move in with her and accompany her to work."

Makes logical sense. "And?"

"She refused. Then I decided I'd prefer for her to be away

from Denver, out of her normal routine in case anyone has been watching." After a moment's hesitation, Hawkeye slid the snapshot onto the table, facedown.

Hawkeye knew every one of Jacob's weaknesses. If he glanced at Elissa's face, the job would become personal. She wouldn't be a random woman he could ignore.

Jacob looked across the expanse of the room, at the two men talking trash at the nearby pool table. Above them, a neon beer sign dangled from a tired-looking nail. The paint was peeling from the shabby wall, and the red glare from the light made the atmosphere all the more depressing.

"Her parents own a pub. Right now, she's running it on their behalf while they're back home in Ireland for a well-deserved vacation. Her father has just recovered from a bout with cancer, and they're celebrating his recovery."

Of course Hawkeye crafted a compelling narrative. He knew how to motivate people, be it through their heartstrings or sense of justice. At times, he'd stoke anger. His ability to get people to do what he wanted was his biggest strength as well as his greatest failing.

Never had his powers of persuasion been more on display than when he'd gotten his Army Ranger team out of Peru, despite the overwhelming odds.

From the beginning, the mission had been FUBAR—fucked up beyond all recognition. They sustained enough casualties to decimate even the strongest and bravest. Relentlessly Hawkeye had urged each soldier on. Despite his own injuries, Hawkeye had carried one man miles to the extraction point.

What happened immediately after that would haunt Hawkeye and Jacob to the end of their days, and it created a bond each would take to the grave.

"You've had some time on the ranch. I assume you're a hundred percent?"

Physically, yes. But part of him would always be in that South American jungle, trying to figure out what had gone so horribly fucking wrong.

Hawkeye nudged the photograph a little closer to Jacob.

"Who is she to you?"

Hawkeye hesitated long enough to capture Jacob's interest.

"Someone I used to know."

Jacob studied his friend intently. "Used to?"

Hawkeye shrugged. "It was a long time ago. Right after we got back from Peru." He stared at the photo. "She helped me through the rough patch."

Tension made Hawkeye's voice rough, and he cleared his throat.

"Shit." Jacob cursed himself for not walking out the moment Hawkeye asked for help. "It—whatever it was between you—is in the past?"

"Yeah. She's a smart woman, recognized damaged goods and was astute enough not to follow when I walked away." He shrugged. "To tell the truth, she's too damn good for me. We both knew it."

"It's over?"

"There never was anything significant. She's a friend. Nothing more. But if anyone's intent on hurting me…" With great deliberation, Hawkeye flipped over the picture.

Jacob couldn't help himself. He looked.

The woman was breathtaking. She was seated on a white-painted carousel horse, arms wrapped around its shiny brass pole. Dark, wavy hair teased her shoulders. But it was her eyes that stopped him cold.

He was a practical man more accustomed to making life-and-death decisions than indulging in fanciful poetry, but that particular shade of blue made him think of the columbines that carpeted the ranch's meadow each summer.

Her smile radiated a joy that he wasn't sure he'd ever experienced. Longing—hot and swift—ripped through him. Ruthlessly he shoved the unfamiliar emotion away. He was seated across from Hawkeye, discussing a job. Nothing more. If he accepted the assignment, it would be his responsibility to keep her safe and ensure she had plenty to smile about in the future.

"After this, Commander Walker, we'll call it even."

"Even from you, that's a fucking cheap shot." Jacob didn't need the reminder of how much he owed Hawkeye. Nothing would ever be *even* after the way the man rescued Jacob's mother from the inside of a Mexican jail cell.

Unable to stop himself, Jacob picked up the photo. Hawkeye's gamble—his drive deep into the Colorado mountains—had paid off. Jacob couldn't walk away. Elissa wasn't a random client. She was a woman who'd shown compassion to Hawkeye, and that shouldn't have put her at risk.

With a silent vow that he'd care for her until the shitstorm passed, Jacob tucked the picture inside his shirt pocket.

Hawkeye lifted his shot glass, then downed his whiskey in a single swallow.

———

"Sir? It's closing time." Elissa summoned a false, I'm-not-exhausted smile for the cowboy sitting alone at a table for two in her mom and dad's Denver-area pub. The man had been there for hours, his back to the wall. From time to time, he'd glance at the baseball game on the television, but for the most part, he watched other customers coming and going. More than once, she was aware of his focused gaze on her as she worked.

When he arrived, he asked for a soda water with lime.

Nothing stronger. Minutes before the kitchen closed, he ordered the pub's famous fish and chips.

Throughout the evening, he hadn't engaged with her attempts at conversation, and he paid his bill—in cash, with a generous tip—before last call.

Now he was the last remaining customer, and she wanted him to leave so she could lock up, head for home. She needed a long, hot bath, doused with a generous helping of her favorite lavender Epsom salts.

If she were lucky, she'd fall asleep quickly and manage a few hours of deep sleep before the alarm shrieked, dragging her out of bed. After all, she still had to run her own business while taking care of the bar.

Over the past few days, exhaustion had made her mentally plan a vacation, far away from Colorado. Maybe a remote tropical island where she could rest and bask in the sun. A swim-up bar would be nice, and so would a beachside massage beneath a palm tree.

But she was still stuck in reality. She had to complete the closing checklist, and that meant dispensing with the final, reluctant-to-leave guest.

With a forced half smile, she tried again. "Sir?"

The man tipped the brim of his cowboy hat, allowing her to get a good look at his face.

She pressed her hand to her mouth to stifle a gasp.

He was gorgeous. Not just classically handsome, but drop-dead, movie star gorgeous.

His square jaw was shadowed with stubble, but that enhanced the sharpness of his features. And his eyes… They were bright green, reminding her of a malachite gemstone she'd seen in a tourist shop.

In a leisurely perusal, he swept his gaze up her body, starting with her sensible shoes, then moving up her thighs, taking in the curve of her hips, then the swell of her suddenly aching breasts.

When their gazes met, she was helplessly ensnared, riveted by his intensity.

The silence stretched, and she cleared her throat. She was usually a total professional, accustomed to dealing with loners, as well as groups out celebrating and being rowdy, or even the occasional customer in search of a therapist while drowning their sorrows. But this raw, physical man left her twitterpated, her pulse racing while her imagination soared on hungry, sexual wings.

Andrew, the barback, switched off some of the lights, jolting her. After shaking her head, she asserted herself. "It's closing time, sir."

"Yes, ma'am." The cowboy stood, the legs of his chair scraping against the wooden floor. "I'll be going, then."

His voice was deep and rich, resonating through her. It invited trust even as it hinted at intimacy.

An involuntary spark of need raced up her spine.

Forcing herself to ignore it, she followed him to the exit. Instead of leaving, he paused.

They stood so close that she inhaled his scent, that of untamed open spaces. She tried to move away but was rooted to the spot. She was ensnared by his masculine force field—an intoxicating mixture of raw dominance and constrained power.

Desire lay like smoke in his eyes. In a response as old as time, pheromones stampeded through her. She ached to know him, to feel his strong arms wrap around her, to have his hips grinding against hers as he claimed her hard.

Dear God, what is wrong with me?

It had been too long since she'd been with a lover, but this cowboy was the type of man who'd turn her inside out if she let him. And she was too smart for that.

"Ma'am." Finally he thumbed the brim of his hat in a casual, respectful farewell that made her wonder if she'd imagined what had just happened between them.

"Thanks for coming in." Her response was automatic.

"I'll see you soon." Conviction as well as promise laced his words, and it shocked her how much she hoped he meant it.

After locking the door behind him, she stood in place for a few moments, watching him climb into his nondescript black pickup truck. It resembled a thousand others on the road, in stark contrast to its intense, unforgettable owner.

The barback tugged the chain to turn off the Open sign, reminding her of the chores still ahead of her.

It was past time to shove away thoughts of the stranger.

She checked her watch. A few minutes after one a.m.

It had been a long day. *Another* long day. With her parents still on vacation, the responsibility for running the pub had fallen to her. That wouldn't have been so bad, but Mary, the nighttime manager, had called in sick. And Elissa's freelance graphic project was due at the end of the week. Sleep had been in short supply for the past month.

Month?

Actually, it had been more than a year. Her father's cancer diagnosis had upended her family's world. The emotional turmoil had taken its toll as they all fought through the terrifying uncertainty and fear.

After his final chemotherapy treatment, her parents had departed for a much-needed break.

Andrew continued walking through the area, switching off the neon beer signs. "Everything's done. Clean and ready for tomorrow."

"Not sure how I would have managed without you." For the first time ever, he'd ended up waiting on several customers, and he'd done a good job. "Why don't you go ahead and leave?"

"I'll wait until you're done and walk you to your car."

"That's okay." She shook her head. It had been busier than usual for a Tuesday, more like she'd expect closer to the weekend. "I still have to reconcile the cash register, and that will take some time. You worked your ass off this evening. Go see your girlfriend."

"It's our one-month date-iversary. I didn't know that was a thing until this morning, and she warned me I better not screw it up." Clearly besotted, he grinned. "I don't mind staying, though, for a few more minutes."

"Go."

He glanced toward the rear exit. "If you're sure…"

"It's your date-iversary. *Go.*" She made a sweeping motion with her hand.

Grinning, she turned the deadbolt once he left.

After turning off the main dining room lights, Elissa retreated to the tiny management office. She sank into the old military-surplus style leather chair behind the metal desk. Determined to ignore the clock on the wall, she counted the cash, balanced the register, then ran the credit card settlement.

Once everything was done and the bank deposit was locked in the safe, she sighed, part in relief, part in satisfaction.

Finally.

As usual, she straightened the desktop and gave the office a final glance to be sure everything was where it needed to be.

Satisfied, she released her hair from its ponytail and fed her fingers through the strands to separate them, part of her ritual for ending the workday and easing into her off time.

Then she reached for her lightweight jacket. Even though it was summer, Colorado could still hold a chill after the sun set. Finally she slung her purse over her shoulder before plucking her keyring from a hook in the wall.

She let herself out the door, then secured the deadbolt behind her.

There were only a handful of vehicles in the parking lot, and she headed toward hers at a quick clip.

As she neared it, a figure detached itself from the adjoining building.

She struggled for calm, telling herself that the person wasn't heading toward her. But as she broke into a jog, so did the figure.

Frantically she ran, hitting the remote control to unlock the car, praying she could make it to safety before the assailant reached her. As she grasped the door handle, he crowded behind her, pressing her against the side of the vehicle.

"Get away from me!"

When he didn't, she screamed.

"Calm down."

Fuck. She recognized his gruff voice. *The cowboy.* For a moment, she went still. But when he pressed her harder against the car, fear flared, and she instinctively fought back. "Get the hell off me!"

He was unyielding, and her strength was no match for his.

"Hawkeye sent me."

Elissa froze. *Hawkeye?*

Of course he'd sent someone. She should have expected it when she refused to let him provide her with a bodyguard.

Years before, she'd met the wounded military man when he returned from an overseas mission. The first few times he'd come into the pub, he'd been quiet, drinking whiskey neat, staring at a wall while occasionally flinching.

They'd gone out a number of times, and she'd cared about

him. But no matter how hard she tried, she couldn't connect with him on an emotional level. He kept more secrets than he shared. But the one thing she learned was that the need for revenge consumed his every waking thought. In the end, it had been impossible to have any kind of relationship with him.

When he informed her that he'd started Hawkeye Security, she wasn't surprised. And when he came to say goodbye, she tearfully stroked his cheek while wishing him well.

She had been stunned when he called her to tell her she was at risk. Someone from his past threatened the people he cared about. Before hanging up, she dismissed his ridiculous concerns. Their halfhearted relationship was so far in the past that no one could possibly believe that she meant anything to Hawkeye.

"You're going to need to come with me."

"Oh hell no." Her earlier attraction to the stranger had vanished, replaced by anger. She made her own choices and didn't appreciate his heavy-handed tactics. "Tell Hawkeye I said both of you should fuck off. Or better yet, I will."

"I'm not sure you understand." His breath was warm and threatening next to her ear.

And now she understood why he'd spent so many hours at that table. He'd been studying her, planning the best way to bend her to his will.

But Elissa answered to no man.

"You're in danger."

"I can take care of myself. Now get off me, you..." *What?* "Oaf."

"As soon as you give me your word that you'll get in my truck without creating a fuss."

Realizing physical resistance was futile, she allowed her body to go limp and concentrated on tamping down her adrenaline long enough to outwit him. She needed to think and escape his unbearable presence. "How about I'll go home and stay there?"

"Not happening."

"Look…" There was no way she would yield to this over-size, determined goon, even if he was pure masculine perfection. "I'll agree to have one of his employees stay with me."

"He made that offer. You turned it down."

Damn you both. Why hadn't she just agreed to Hawkeye's suggestions?

"Let me be clear, Elissa…"

Despite herself, the way he said her name, gently curled around the sibilant sound, made her nerves tingle.

"He made it my job to protect you, and he signed off on my plan."

"Care to fill me in?"

"Yeah. We'll go to my ranch until he gives the all-clear."

Unnerved, she shivered. "Ranch?" That was worse than she could have imagined, and fresh panic set in. "I demand to talk to Hawkeye this instant."

"Demand all you want, little lady."

She refused to leave town, the pub, and be somewhere remote for an indeterminate amount of time with the cowboy shadowing her twenty-four seven. "No. No." She shook her head. "It's impossible. I'm needed here. And Hawkeye knows it." Struggling for breath, she pushed back against him. "We can work something out, I'm sure."

"You can take it up with him."

"Now we're getting somewhere. Let me get my phone out of my purse." *And figure out how to get in my car and drive like hell.*

"Not until we're on the road." He looped his massive hands around her much smaller wrists and drew them behind her.

"Ouch! Release me immediately!"

Though he didn't hurt her, his grip was uncompromising. "As soon as you agree to get in my truck without struggling."

"Look, Mr.—" *God. I don't know your name.* And like the asshole he was, he didn't fill in the missing information.

"We're done talking."

She stamped her foot on his instep, and he didn't even grunt, frustrating the hell out of her.

"Please get in my truck, Elissa."

Since he was immovable, she tried another approach, pleading with his better self. "I'm begging you. Don't do this. Let me go home." Elissa turned her head, trying to see him over her shoulder. Because of his hat and the darkness of the moonless and cloud-filled sky, his expression was unreadable. "You can follow me to my place." The lie easily rolled off her tongue. Anything to get away.

"Within the next five seconds, you'll be given two options, Ms. Conroy. One, you can come with me willingly."

"And the other?"

"You can come with me unwillingly."

"Option C. None of the above." With all her might, she shoved back, but he tightened his grip to the point of hurting her.

As if on cue, a big black truck—his, no doubt—pulled into view. Since he didn't react, it obviously meant Hawkeye had sent more than one person to deal with her. "This is absurd."

The vehicle, with no lights on, pulled to a stop nearby.

"I'll need your keys, Ms. Conroy."

She shook her head in defiance.

"Always going to do things the hard way?"

Since he was still holding her wrists, it was ridiculously easy for him to pry apart her fingers and take the fob from her.

"Has anyone ever told you that you're annoying as hell?"

A woman slid from the cab of the still-running pickup

183

and left the driver's side door open a crack. A gentle chime echoed around them, while light spilled from the interior, allowing Elissa to make out a few of the new arrival's features.

Dressed all in black, she was about the same height and build as Elissa. She even had long dark hair.

"Perimeter is still clear." Then in a cheery voice, she went on. "I see you haven't lost your way with the ladies, Commander."

He growled, all alpha male and frustration. "You're here to help, Fagan."

"That's exactly what I'm doing."

The cowboy eased his hold a little.

"Sorry for the caveman's actions, ma'am. I'm Agent Kayla Fagan. And I'm afraid Commander Walker needs a remedial training class in diplomacy."

Walker. First name? Or last? "Diplomacy? Is that what you call an abduction?"

He remained implacable. "I have my orders, and Ms. Conroy wasn't interested in talking."

Bastard. "His behavior needs to be reported to Hawkeye."

"I'll let you do that yourself," Kayla replied. "But honestly, I'd like to listen in."

"Get out of here, Fagan." He kept his body against hers while somehow managing to toss her keys to Kayla.

"Wait! You look so much like me you could be my double."

"That's the plan. Fagan will make it appear as if you're following your normal routine this evening while we get away. When we're on the road, you can talk to Hawkeye and make a strategic plan for opening the bar." Walker's tone was uncompromising.

The infuriating men had planned out everything.

Kayla opened the car door and slid into the driver's seat.

"Time's up, ma'am."

"Could you be any more condescending?"

"As I said, we can do this the hard way or the easy way. Your choice."

Determinedly Elissa set her chin. "I'm not going with you."

In a move so calculated and fast that she had no time to react, he took her purse from her, then yanked her around to face him. As if he'd done it a million times, he swept her off her feet, then hauled her into the air.

The Neanderthal tossed her over his shoulder, and she landed against his rigid body with so much force that breath rushed out of her lungs, stunning her into silence.

"The hard way it is."

Read more of Hold On To Me.

ABOUT THE AUTHOR

I invite you to be the very first to know all the news by subscribing to my very special VIP Reader newsletter! You'll find exclusive excerpts, bonus reads, and insider information. https://www.sierracartwright.com/subscribe/

For tons of fun and to meet other awesome people like you, join my Facebook reader group: https://www.facebook.-com/groups/SierrasSuperStars And for a current booklist, please visit my website www.sierracartwright.com

International bestselling author Sierra Cartwright was born in England, and she spent her early childhood traipsing through castles and dreaming of happily-ever afters. She was raised in Colorado and now calls Galveston, Texas home. She loves to connect with her readers, so please feel free to drop her a note.

facebook.com/SierraCartwrightOfficial
instagram.com/sierracartwrightauthor
bookbub.com/authors/sierra-cartwright

Donovan Dynasty

Bind

Brand

Boss

Mastered

With This Collar

On His Terms

Over The Line

In His Cuffs

For The Sub

In The Den

Made in United States
North Haven, CT
19 November 2021